NANCY DREW

THE NEW CASE FILES

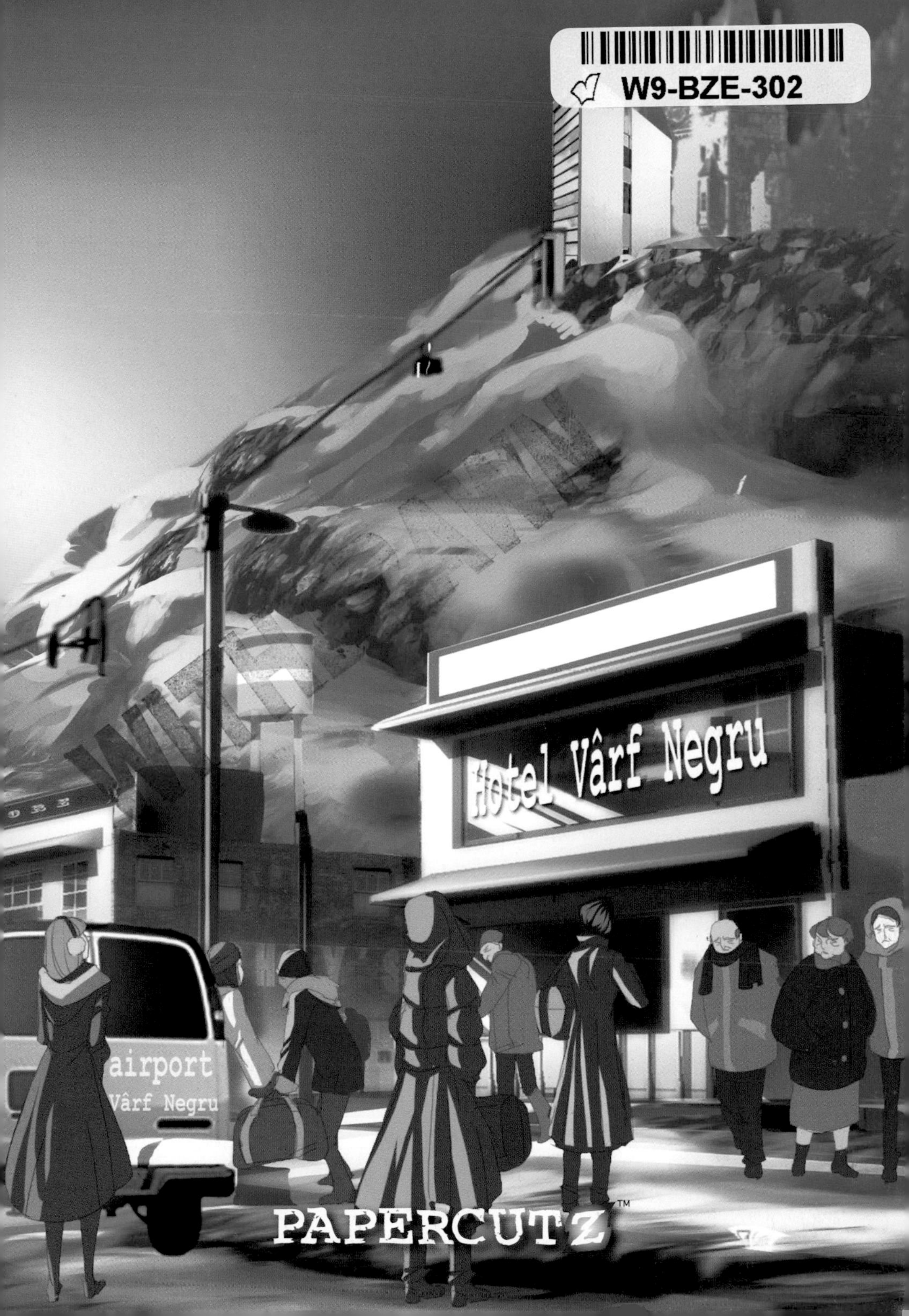
Hotel Vârf Negru
airport
Vârf Negru

PAPERCUTZ™

NANCY DREW GRAPHIC NOVELS AVAILABLE FROM PAPERCUTZ

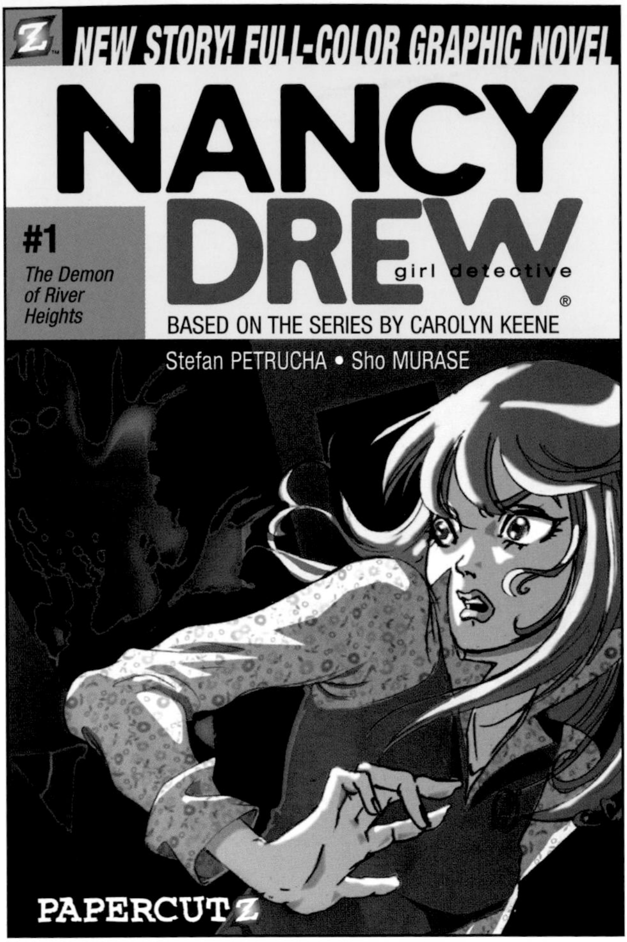
NEW STORY! FULL-COLOR GRAPHIC NOVEL
NANCY DREW
girl detective
#1
The Demon of River Heights
BASED ON THE SERIES BY CAROLYN KEENE
Stefan PETRUCHA • Sho MURASE
PAPERCUTZ

#1 "The Demon of River Heights"

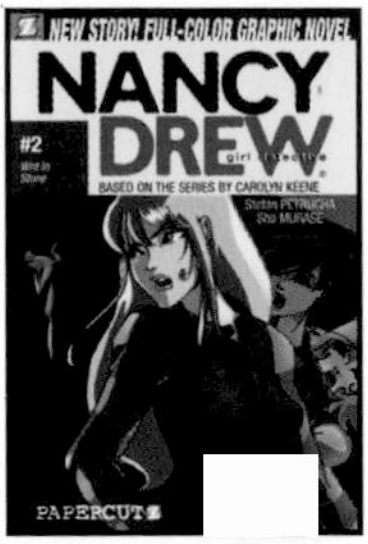
NEW STORY! FULL-COLOR GRAPHIC NOVEL
NANCY DREW
#2
PAPERCUTZ

#2 "Writ In Stone"

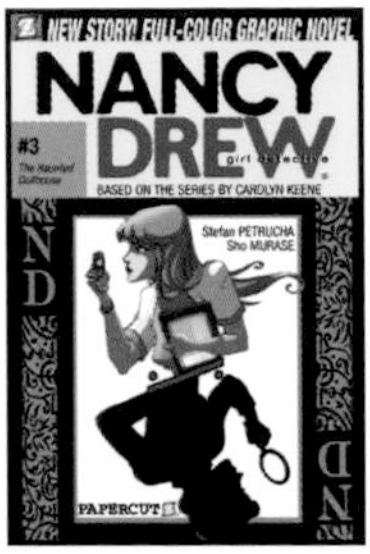
NEW STORY! FULL-COLOR GRAPHIC NOVEL
NANCY DREW
#3
BASED ON THE SERIES BY CAROLYN KEENE
Stefan PETRUCHA
Sho MURASE
PAPERCUTZ

#3 "The Haunted Dollhouse"

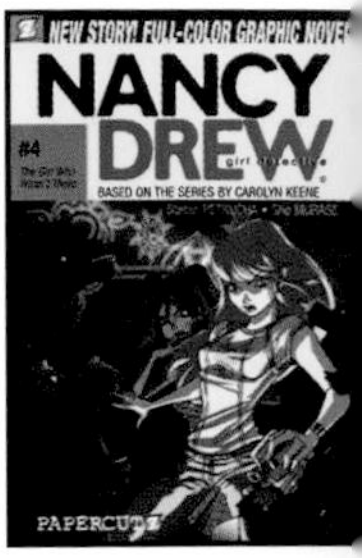
NEW STORY! FULL-COLOR GRAPHIC NOVEL
NANCY DREW
#4
BASED ON THE SERIES BY CAROLYN KEENE
PAPERCUTZ

#4 "The Girl Who Wasn't There"

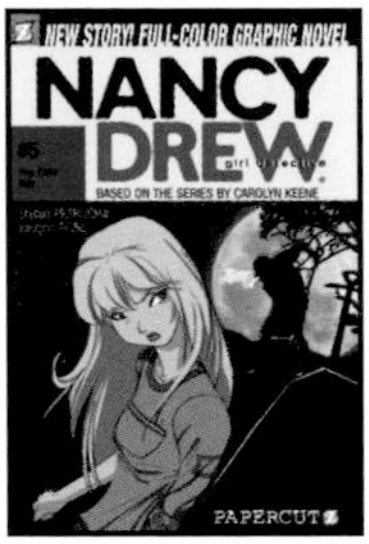
NEW STORY! FULL-COLOR GRAPHIC NOVEL
NANCY DREW
BASED ON THE SERIES BY CAROLYN KEENE
PAPERCUTZ

#5 "The Fake Heir"

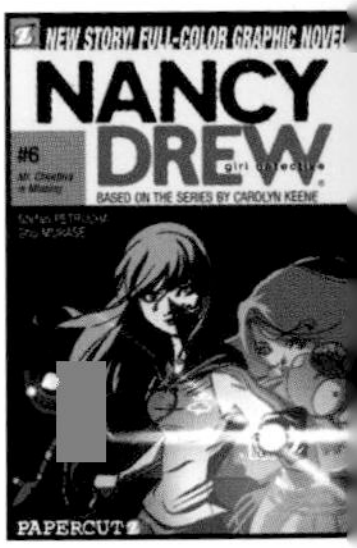
NEW STORY! FULL-COLOR GRAPHIC NOVEL
NANCY DREW
#6
BASED ON THE SERIES BY CAROLYN KEENE
PAPERCUTZ

#6 "Mr. Cheeters Is Missing"

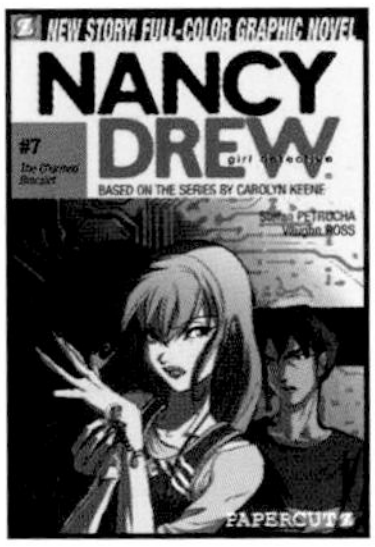
NEW STORY! FULL-COLOR GRAPHIC NOVEL
NANCY DREW
#7
BASED ON THE SERIES BY CAROLYN KEENE
PAPERCUTZ

#7 "The Charmed Bracelet"

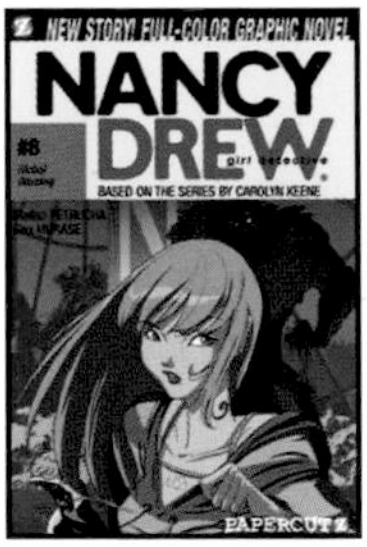
NEW STORY! FULL-COLOR GRAPHIC NOVEL
NANCY DREW
#8
BASED ON THE SERIES BY CAROLYN KEENE
PAPERCUTZ

#8 "Global Warning"

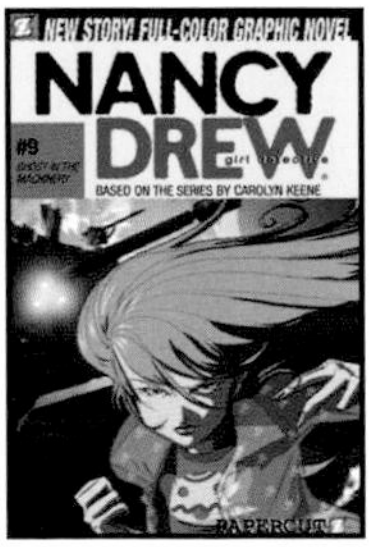
NEW STORY! FULL-COLOR GRAPHIC NOVEL
NANCY DREW
#9
BASED ON THE SERIES BY CAROLYN KEENE
PAPERCUTZ

#9 "Ghost In The Machinery"

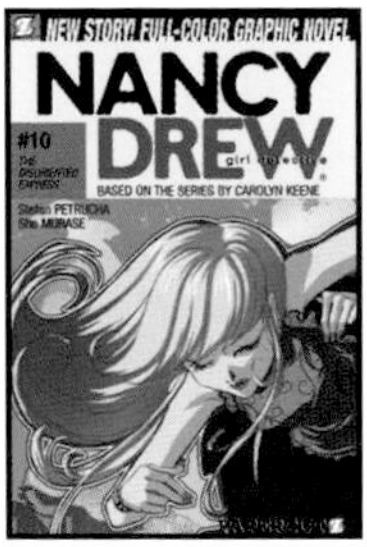
NEW STORY! FULL-COLOR GRAPHIC NOVEL
NANCY DREW
#10
BASED ON THE SERIES BY CAROLYN KEENE
PAPERCUTZ

#10 "The Disoriented Express"

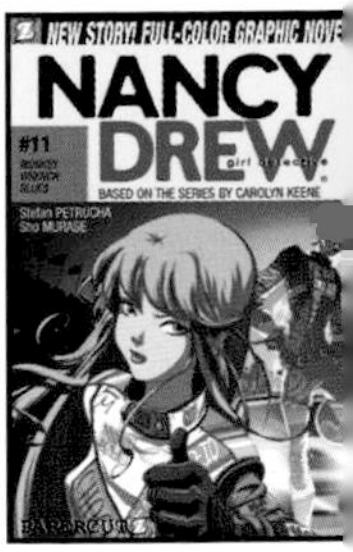
NEW STORY! FULL-COLOR GRAPHIC NOVEL
NANCY DREW
#11
BASED ON THE SERIES BY CAROLYN KEENE
PAPERCUTZ

#11 "Monkey Wrench Blues"

See page 55 for more.

Graphic Novels Are $7.95 in paperback, $12.95 in hardcover.
Available at booksellers everywhere.

Or order from us. Make check payable to NBM Publishing.
Please add $4.00 for postage and handling for the first book, add $1.00 for each additional book.
Send to: Papercutz, 40 Exchange Place, Suite 1308, New York, NY, 10005. 1-800-886-1223.

www.papercutz.com

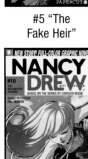

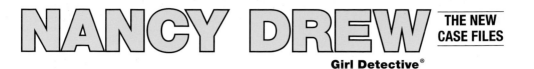

NANCY DREW

THE NEW CASE FILES

Girl Detective®

TOGETHER WITH THE

HARDY BOYS

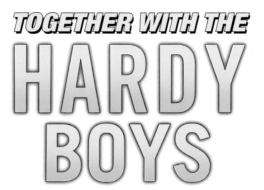

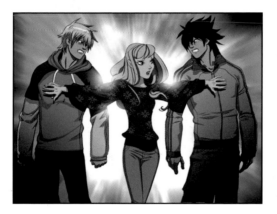

GERRY CONWAY • Writer

based on suggestions by Stephan Petrucha and Sarah Kinney

SHO MURASE • Artist

with 3D CG elenemts and color by CARLOS JOSE GUZMAN

PAULO HENRIQUE, SHO MURASE, CARLOS JOSE GUZMAN • Cover Art

Based on the series by

CAROLYN KEENE

The Hardy Boys characters based on the series by

FRANKLIN W. DIXON

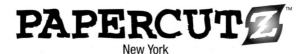

PAPERCUTZ™

New York

Let me introduce myself. I'm Nancy Drew. My friends call me Nancy. My enemies call me a lot of other things better left unsaid. See, I'm a detective. Not really. I mean, I don't have a license or anything. I don't carry a gun (not that I would touch one of those even if I could) or a badge. I'm not even old enough to have one. But I am old enough to know when something isn't right, when somebody's getting an unfair deal, or when someone's done something they shouldn't do. And I know how to stop them, catch them, and get them into the hands of the law, where they belong. I take those things seriously and I'm almost never wrong.

"Together with the Hardy Boys"
GERRY CONWAY – Writer
(Based on suggestions by STEFAN PETRUCHA & SARAH KINNEY)
SHO MURASE — Artist
with 3D CG elements and color by CARLOS JOSE GUZMAN
BRYAN SENKA – Letterer
CHRIS NELSON & SHELLY STERNER – Production
MICHAEL PETRANEK – Associate Editor
JIM SALICRUP
Editor-in-Chief

ISBN: 978-1-59707-262-5 paperback edition
ISBN: 978-1-59707-263-2 hardcover edition

Printed in China.
August 2011 by Asia One Printing LTD.
13/F Asia One Tower
8 Fung Yip St., Chaiwan
Hong Kong

Distributed by Macmillan.

First Printing

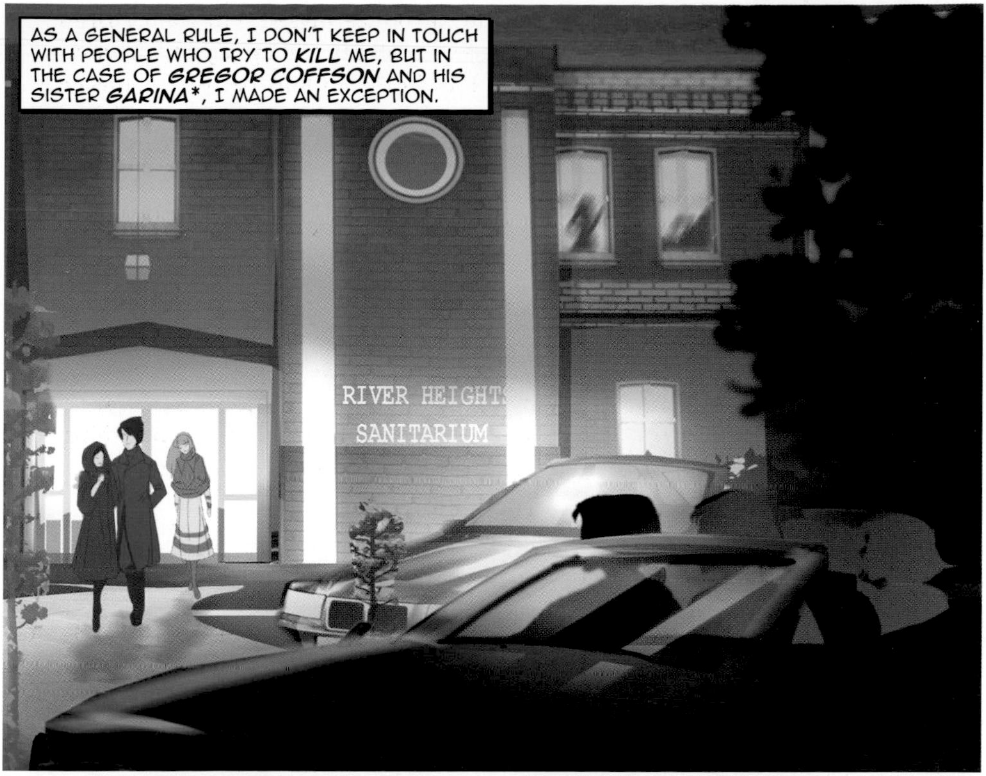
AS A GENERAL RULE, I DON'T KEEP IN TOUCH WITH PEOPLE WHO TRY TO KILL ME, BUT IN THE CASE OF GREGOR COFFSON AND HIS SISTER GARINA*, I MADE AN EXCEPTION.
RIVER HEIGHTS
SANITARIUM

*AS TOLD IN *NANCY DREW THE NEW CASE FILES* #2.

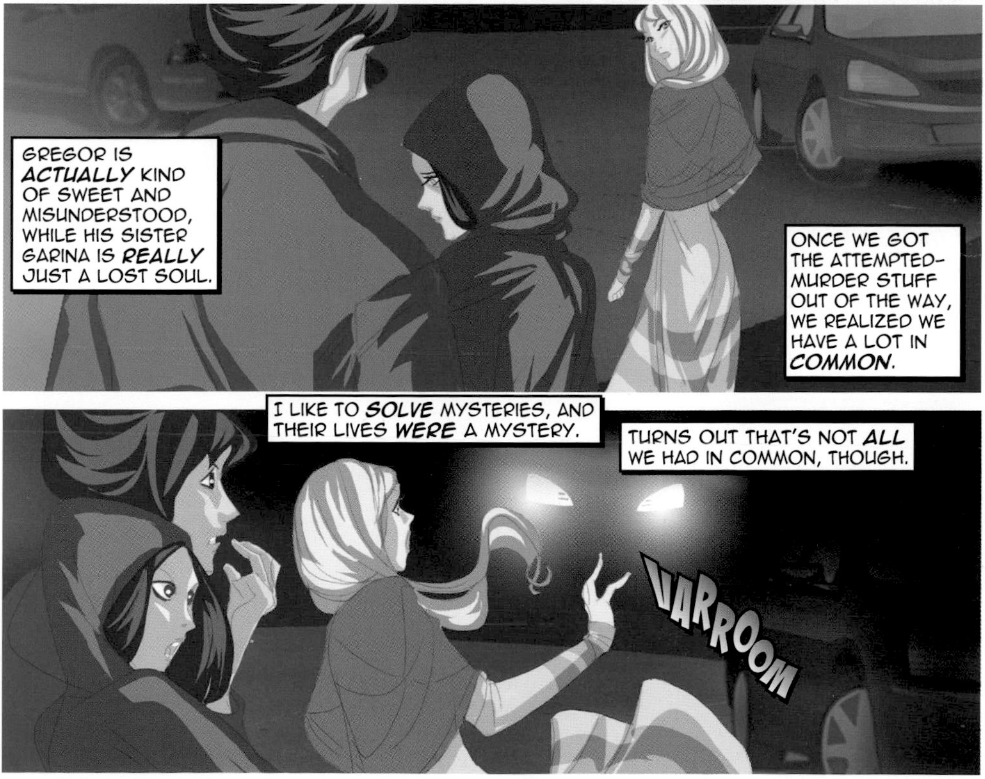
GREGOR IS ACTUALLY KIND OF SWEET AND MISUNDERSTOOD, WHILE HIS SISTER GARINA IS REALLY JUST A LOST SOUL.
ONCE WE GOT THE ATTEMPTED-MURDER STUFF OUT OF THE WAY, WE REALIZED WE HAVE A LOT IN COMMON.
I LIKE TO SOLVE MYSTERIES, AND THEIR LIVES WERE A MYSTERY.
TURNS OUT THAT'S NOT ALL WE HAD IN COMMON, THOUGH.
VARROOM

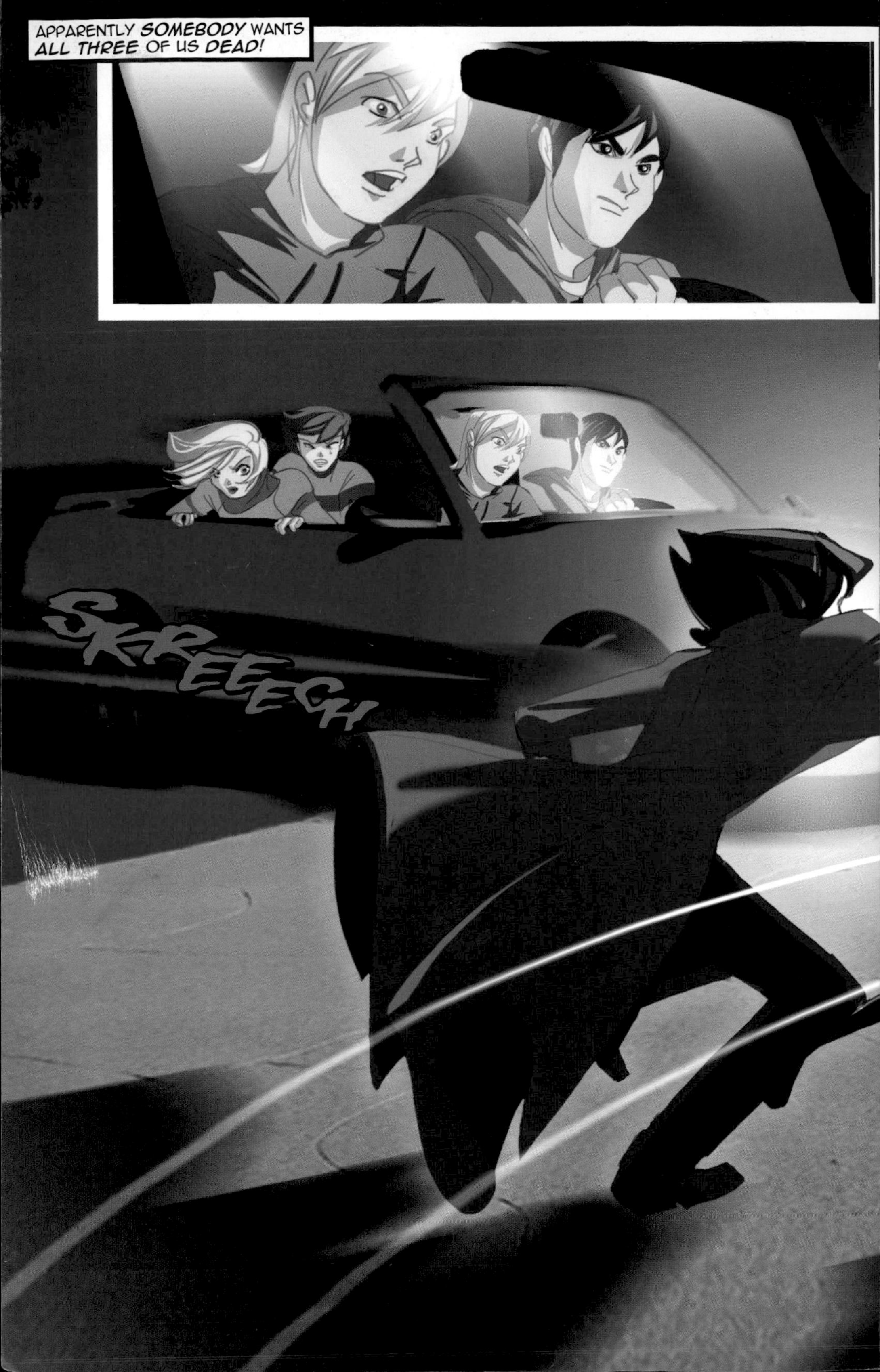

APPARENTLY SOMEBODY WANTS ALL THREE OF US DEAD!
SKREEECH

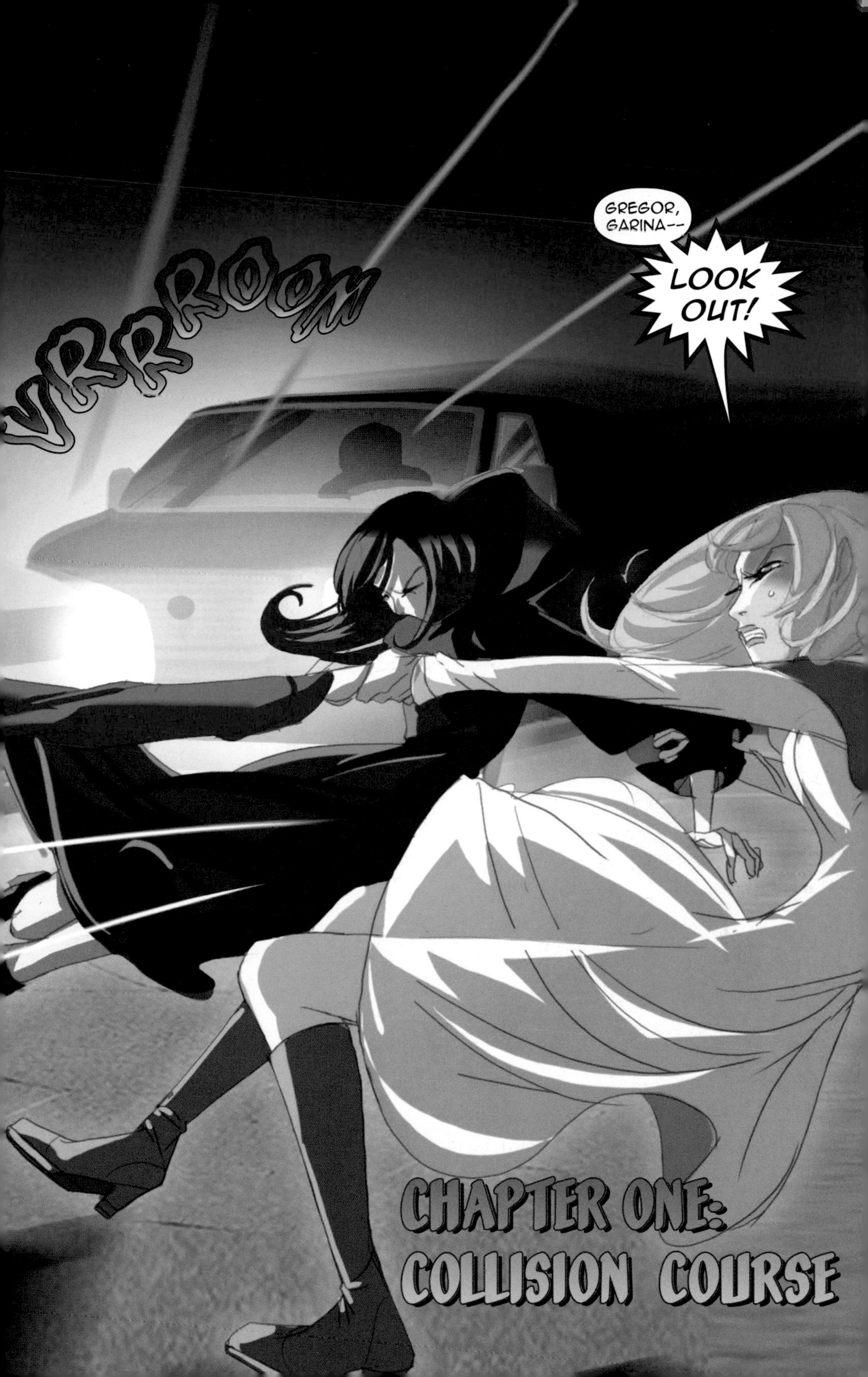
VRRROOM
GREGOR, GARINA--
LOOK OUT!
CHAPTER ONE: COLLISION COURSE

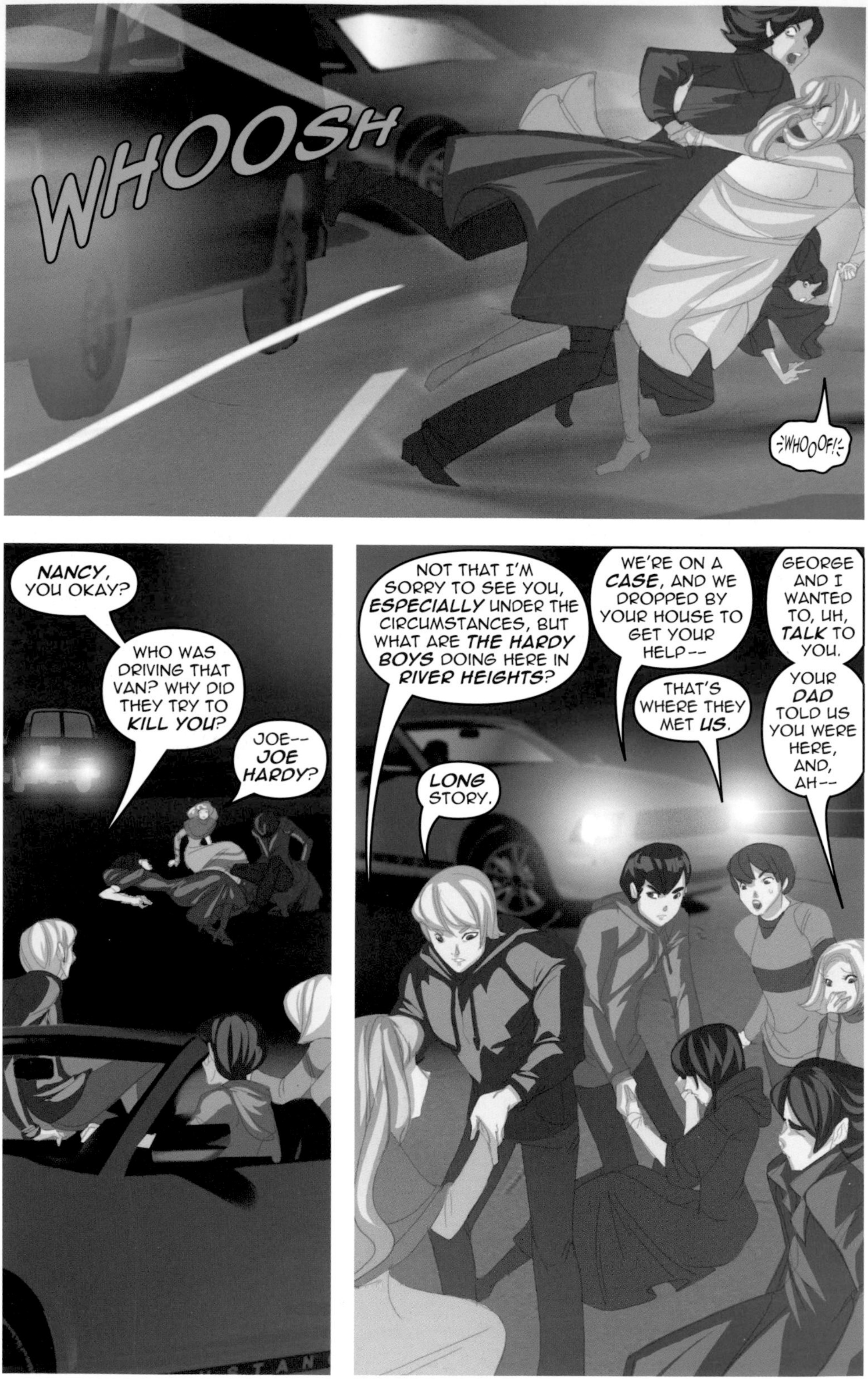
WHOOSH
WHOOOF!
NANCY, YOU OKAY?
WHO WAS DRIVING THAT VAN? WHY DID THEY TRY TO KILL YOU?
JOE-- JOE HARDY?
NOT THAT I'M SORRY TO SEE YOU, ESPECIALLY UNDER THE CIRCUMSTANCES, BUT WHAT ARE THE HARDY BOYS DOING HERE IN RIVER HEIGHTS?
LONG STORY.
WE'RE ON A CASE, AND WE DROPPED BY YOUR HOUSE TO GET YOUR HELP--
THAT'S WHERE THEY MET US.
GEORGE AND I WANTED TO, UH, TALK TO YOU.
YOUR DAD TOLD US YOU WERE HERE, AND, AH--

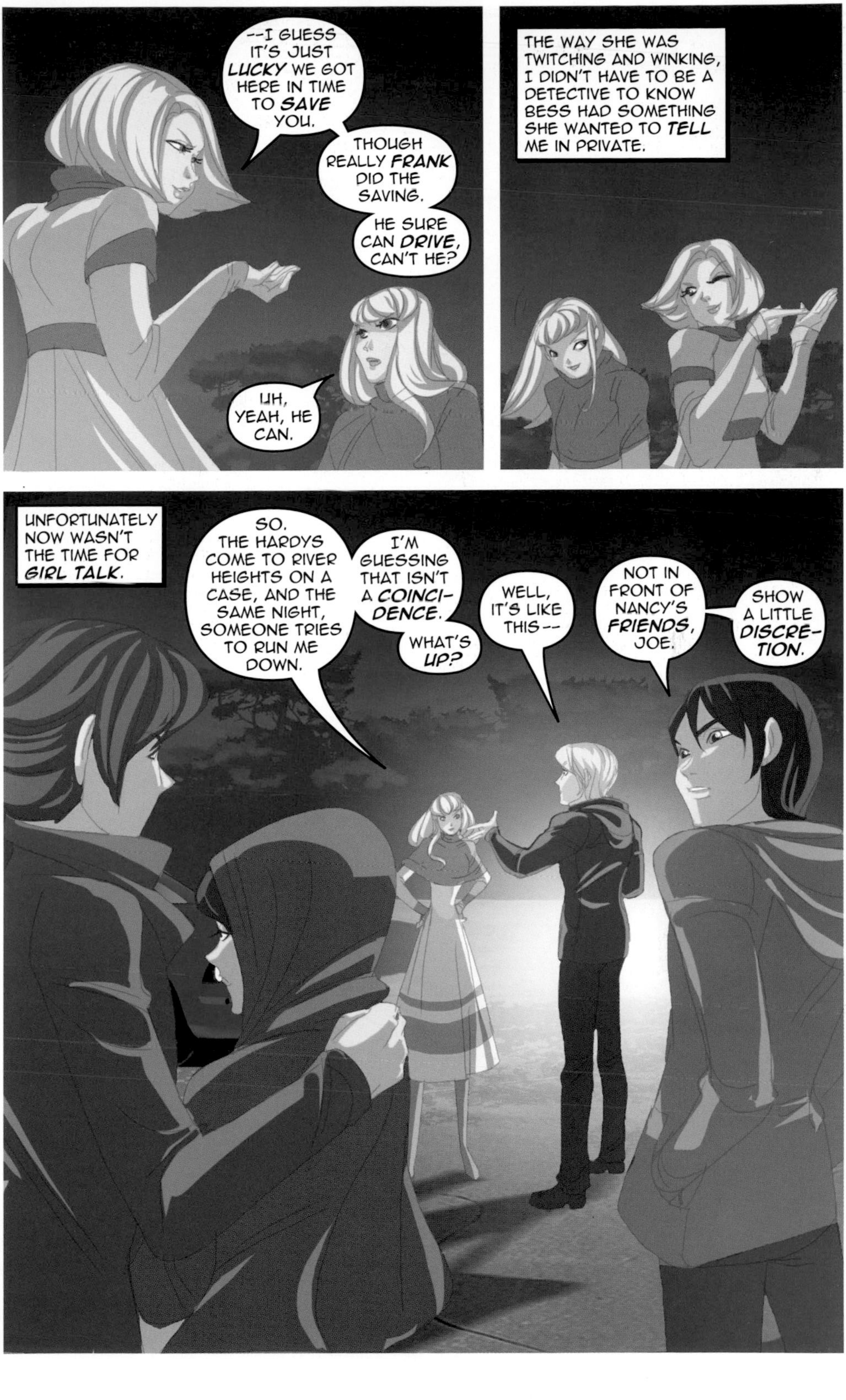
--I GUESS IT'S JUST LUCKY WE GOT HERE IN TIME TO SAVE YOU.
THOUGH REALLY FRANK DID THE SAVING.
HE SURE CAN DRIVE, CAN'T HE?
UH, YEAH, HE CAN.
THE WAY SHE WAS TWITCHING AND WINKING, I DIDN'T HAVE TO BE A DETECTIVE TO KNOW BESS HAD SOMETHING SHE WANTED TO TELL ME IN PRIVATE.
UNFORTUNATELY NOW WASN'T THE TIME FOR GIRL TALK.
SO. THE HARDYS COME TO RIVER HEIGHTS ON A CASE, AND THE SAME NIGHT, SOMEONE TRIES TO RUN ME DOWN.
I'M GUESSING THAT ISN'T A COINCIDENCE.
WHAT'S UP?
WELL, IT'S LIKE THIS--
NOT IN FRONT OF NANCY'S FRIENDS, JOE.
SHOW A LITTLE DISCRETION.

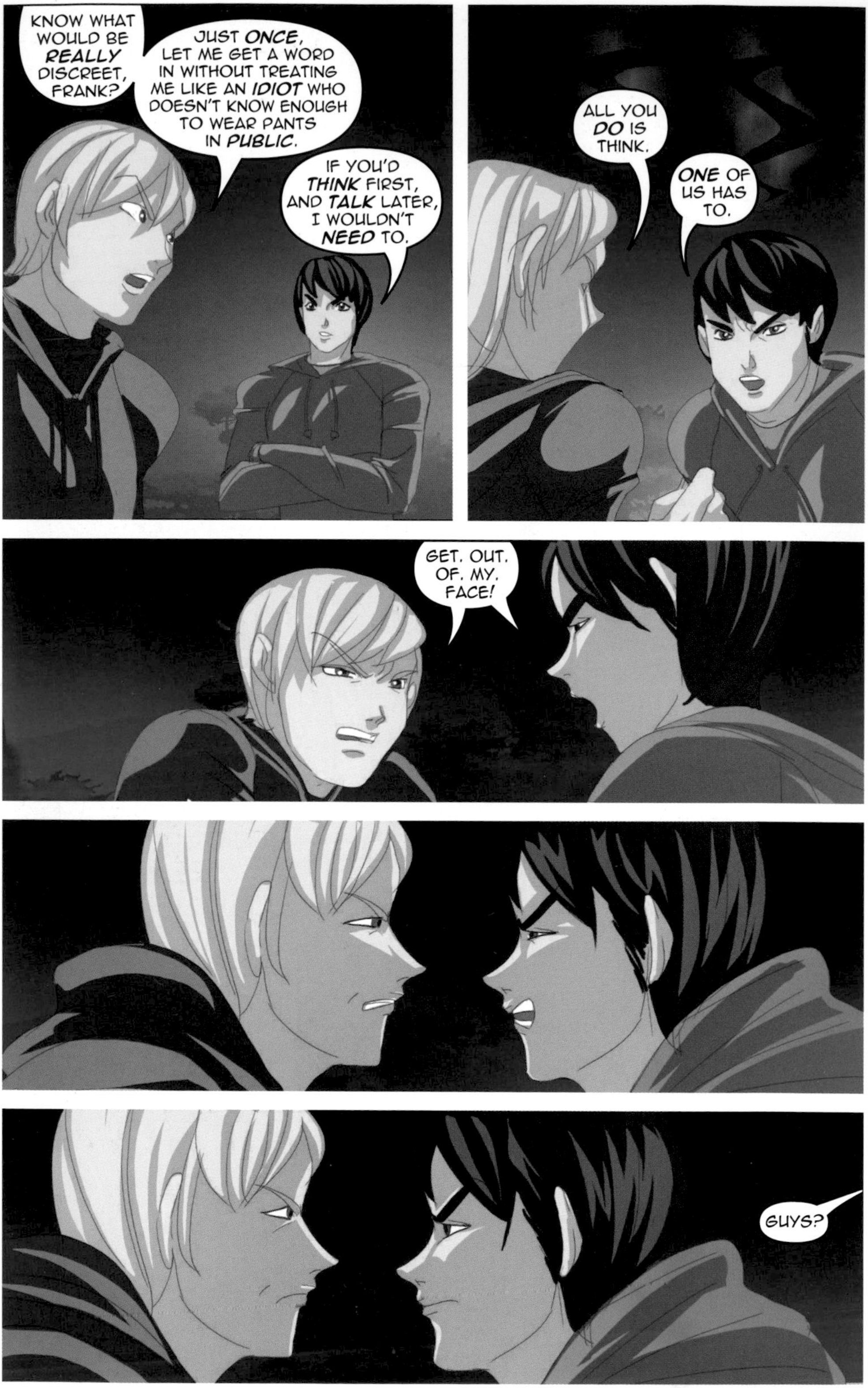
KNOW WHAT WOULD BE REALLY DISCREET, FRANK?
JUST ONCE, LET ME GET A WORD IN WITHOUT TREATING ME LIKE AN IDIOT WHO DOESN'T KNOW ENOUGH TO WEAR PANTS IN PUBLIC.
IF YOU'D THINK FIRST, AND TALK LATER, I WOULDN'T NEED TO.
ALL YOU DO IS THINK.
ONE OF US HAS TO.
GET. OUT. OF. MY. FACE!
GUYS?

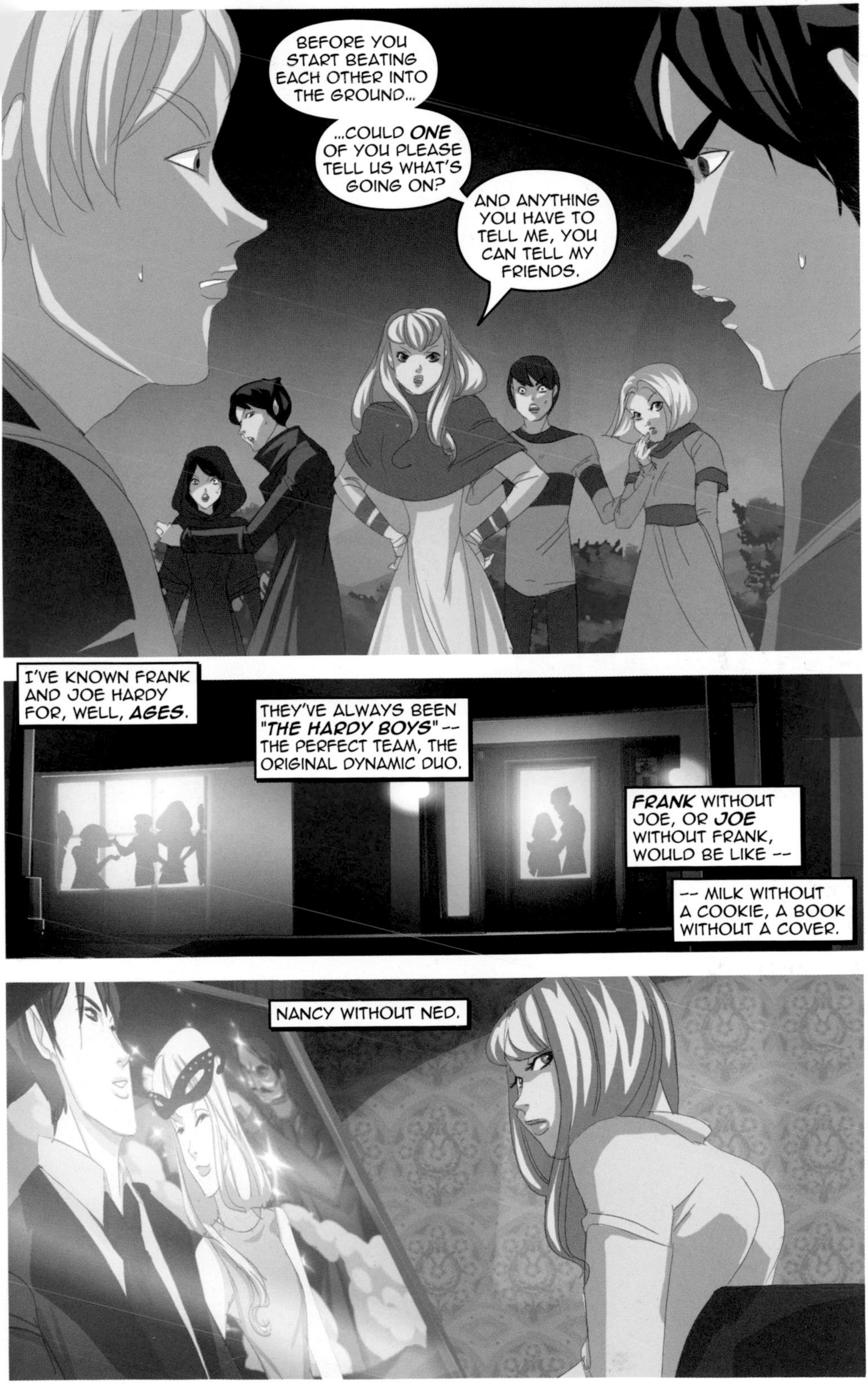
BEFORE YOU START BEATING EACH OTHER INTO THE GROUND...
...COULD ONE OF YOU PLEASE TELL US WHAT'S GOING ON?
AND ANYTHING YOU HAVE TO TELL ME, YOU CAN TELL MY FRIENDS.
I'VE KNOWN FRANK AND JOE HARDY FOR, WELL, AGES.
THEY'VE ALWAYS BEEN "THE HARDY BOYS" -- THE PERFECT TEAM, THE ORIGINAL DYNAMIC DUO.
FRANK WITHOUT JOE, OR JOE WITHOUT FRANK, WOULD BE LIKE --
-- MILK WITHOUT A COOKIE, A BOOK WITHOUT A COVER.
NANCY WITHOUT NED.

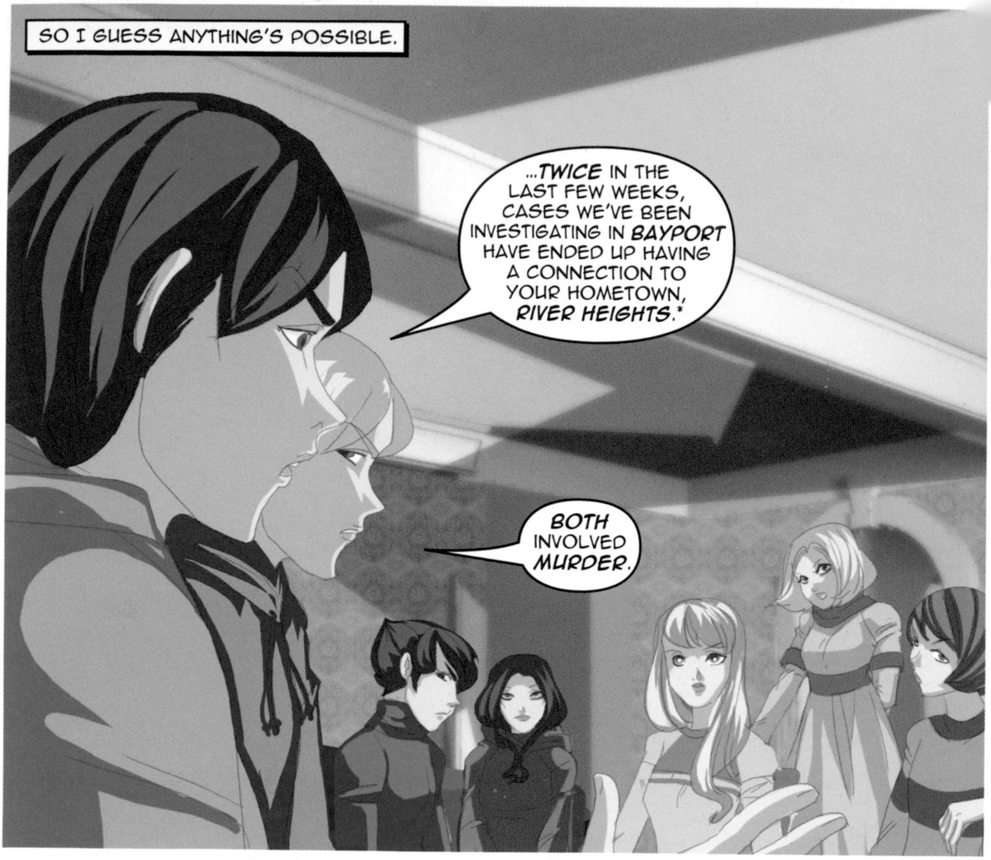
SO I GUESS ANYTHING'S POSSIBLE.
...TWICE IN THE LAST FEW WEEKS, CASES WE'VE BEEN INVESTIGATING IN BAYPORT HAVE ENDED UP HAVING A CONNECTION TO YOUR HOMETOWN, RIVER HEIGHTS.*
BOTH INVOLVED MURDER.

*THE HARDY BOYS THE NEW CASE FILES #1 & #2.

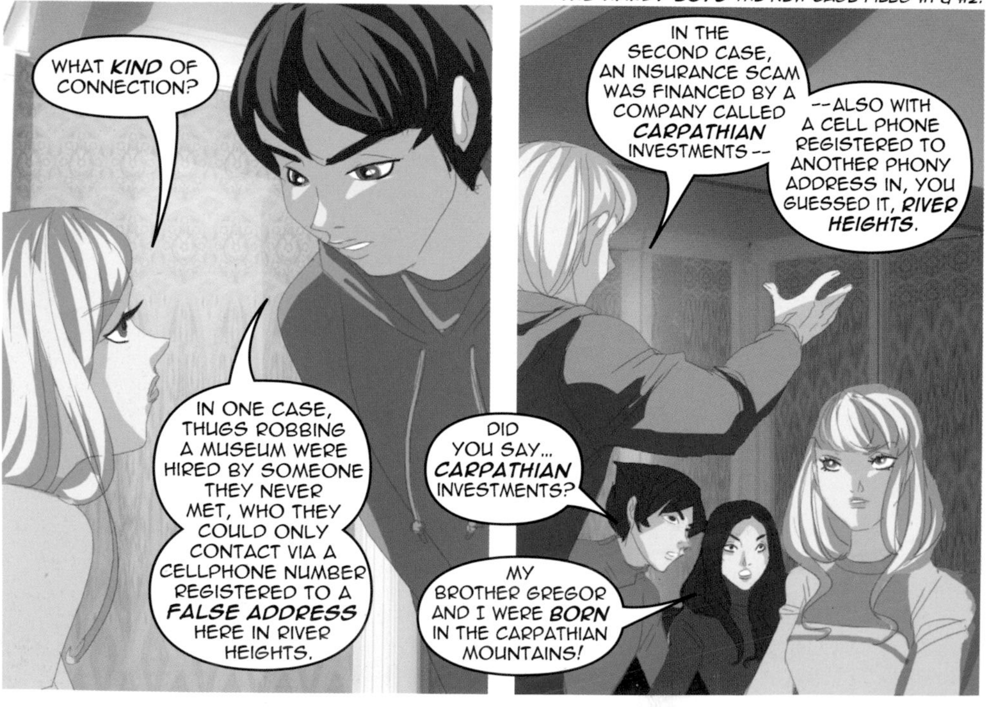
WHAT KIND OF CONNECTION?
IN ONE CASE, THUGS ROBBING A MUSEUM WERE HIRED BY SOMEONE THEY NEVER MET, WHO THEY COULD ONLY CONTACT VIA A CELLPHONE NUMBER REGISTERED TO A FALSE ADDRESS HERE IN RIVER HEIGHTS.
IN THE SECOND CASE, AN INSURANCE SCAM WAS FINANCED BY A COMPANY CALLED CARPATHIAN INVESTMENTS --
--ALSO WITH A CELL PHONE REGISTERED TO ANOTHER PHONY ADDRESS IN, YOU GUESSED IT, RIVER HEIGHTS.
DID YOU SAY... CARPATHIAN INVESTMENTS?
MY BROTHER GREGOR AND I WERE BORN IN THE CARPATHIAN MOUNTAINS!

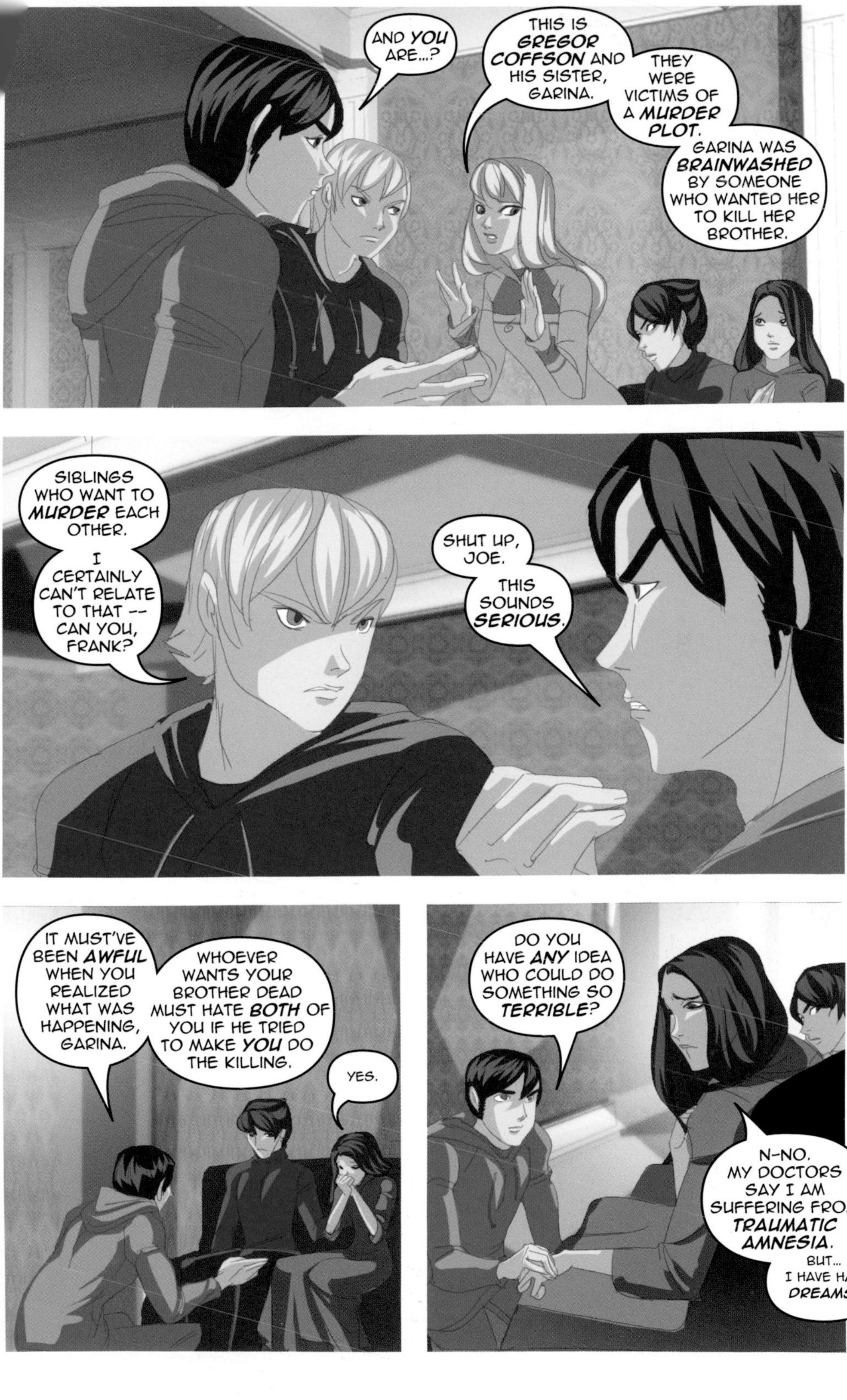
AND YOU ARE...?
THIS IS GREGOR COFFSON AND HIS SISTER, GARINA.
THEY WERE VICTIMS OF A MURDER PLOT.
GARINA WAS BRAINWASHED BY SOMEONE WHO WANTED HER TO KILL HER BROTHER.
SIBLINGS WHO WANT TO MURDER EACH OTHER.
I CERTAINLY CAN'T RELATE TO THAT -- CAN YOU, FRANK?
SHUT UP, JOE.
THIS SOUNDS SERIOUS.
IT MUST'VE BEEN AWFUL WHEN YOU REALIZED WHAT WAS HAPPENING, GARINA.
WHOEVER WANTS YOUR BROTHER DEAD MUST HATE BOTH OF YOU IF HE TRIED TO MAKE YOU DO THE KILLING.
YES.
DO YOU HAVE ANY IDEA WHO COULD DO SOMETHING SO TERRIBLE?
N-NO. MY DOCTORS SAY I AM SUFFERING FROM TRAUMATIC AMNESIA.
BUT... I HAVE HAD DREAMS...

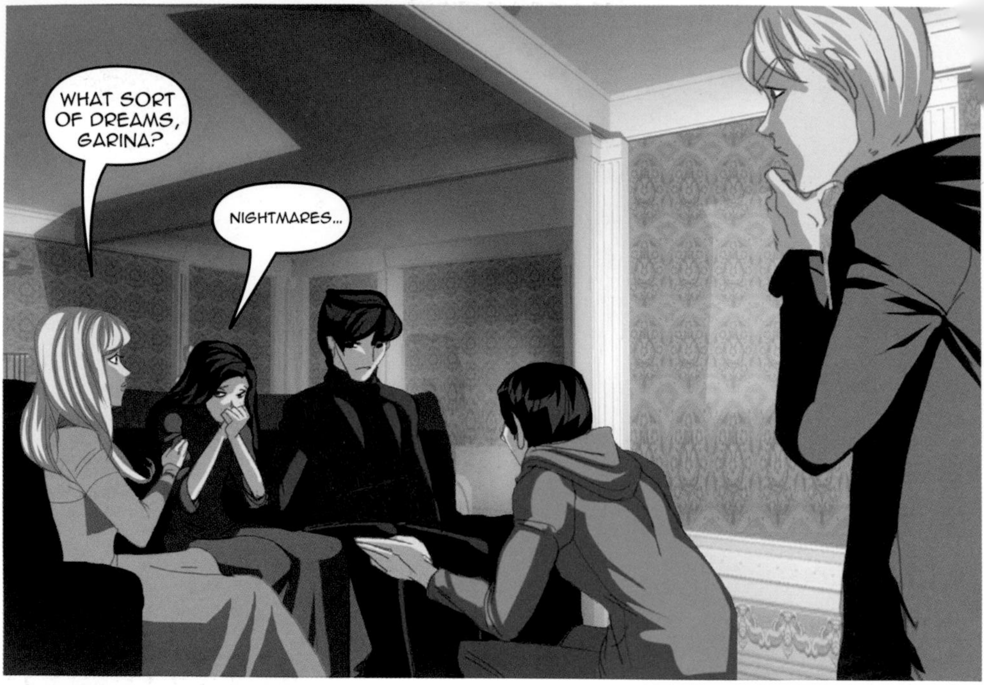
WHAT SORT OF DREAMS, GARINA?
NIGHTMARES...

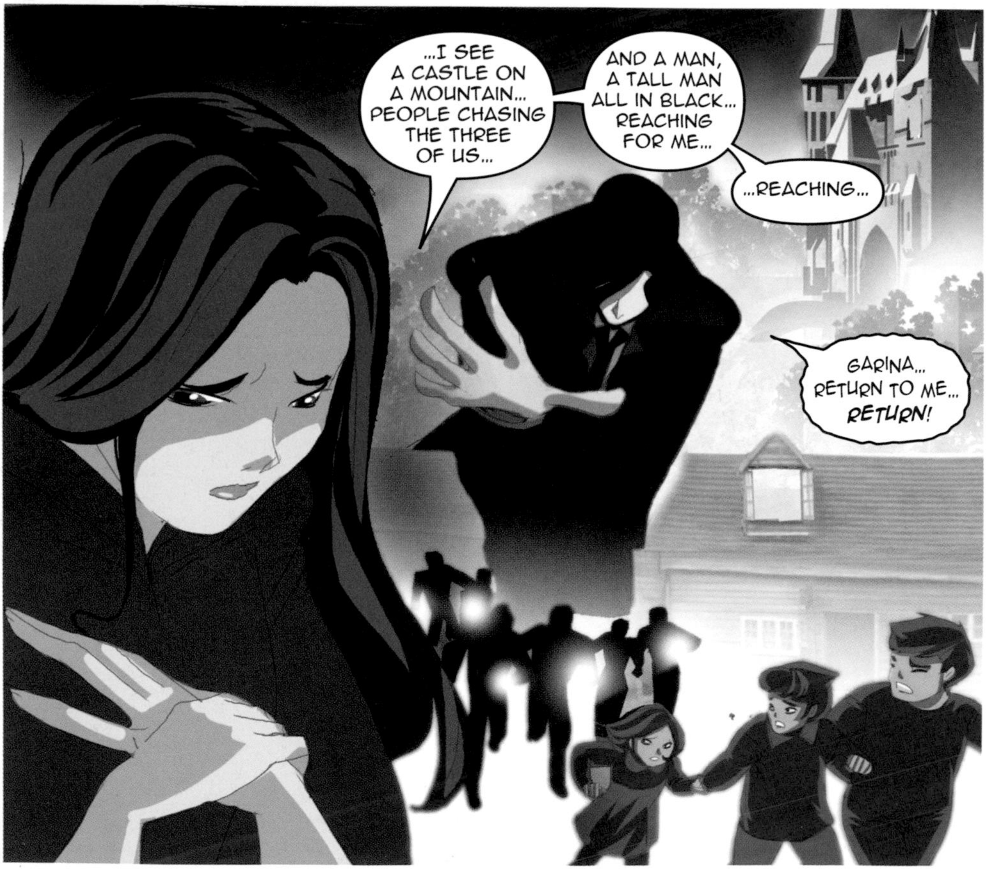
...I SEE A CASTLE ON A MOUNTAIN... PEOPLE CHASING THE THREE OF US...
AND A MAN, A TALL MAN ALL IN BLACK... REACHING FOR ME...
...REACHING...
GARINA... RETURN TO ME... ***RETURN!***

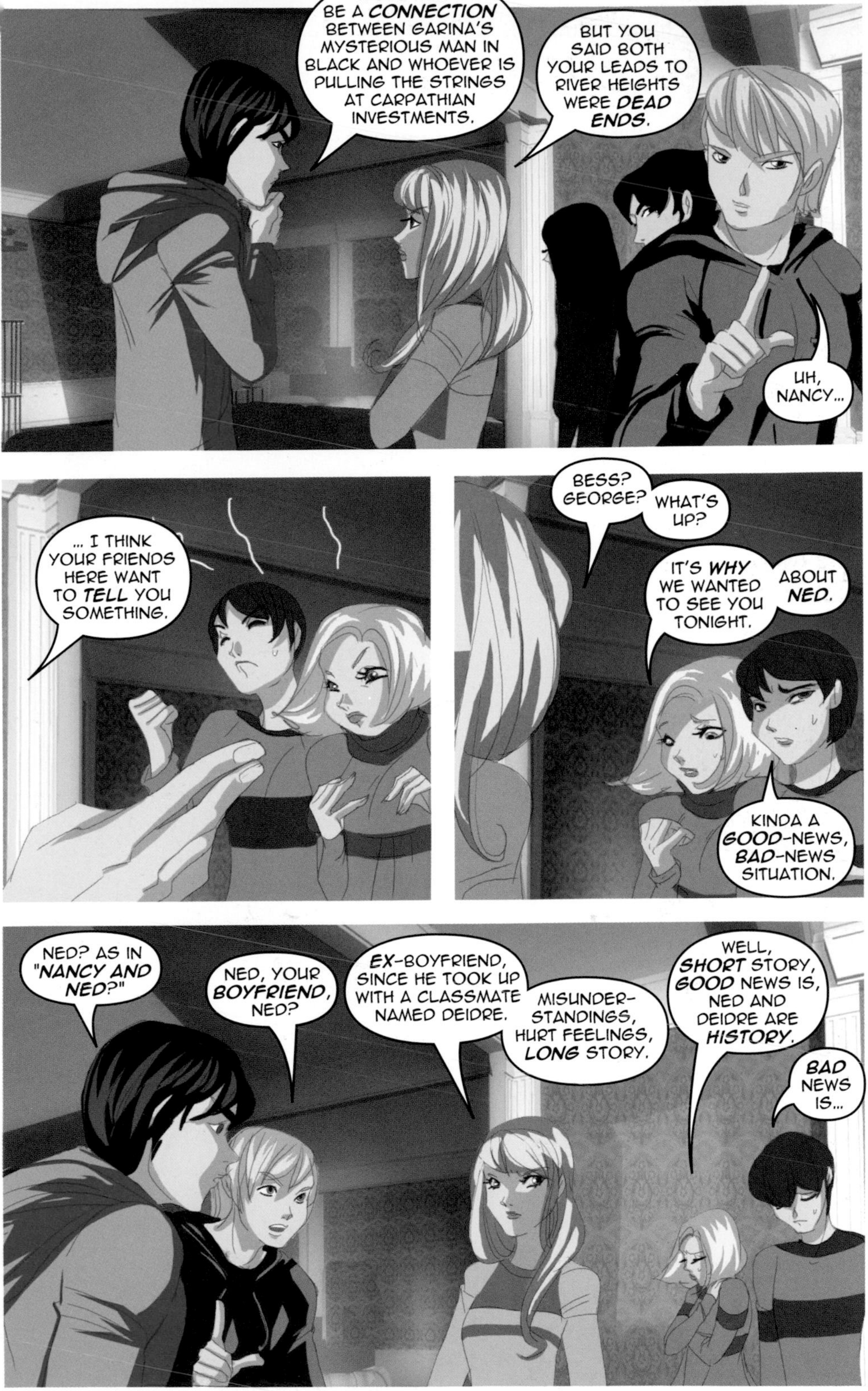
THERE MUST BE A CONNECTION BETWEEN GARINA'S MYSTERIOUS MAN IN BLACK AND WHOEVER IS PULLING THE STRINGS AT CARPATHIAN INVESTMENTS.
BUT YOU SAID BOTH YOUR LEADS TO RIVER HEIGHTS WERE DEAD ENDS.
UH, NANCY...
... I THINK YOUR FRIENDS HERE WANT TO TELL YOU SOMETHING.
BESS? GEORGE?
WHAT'S UP?
IT'S WHY WE WANTED TO SEE YOU TONIGHT.
ABOUT NED.
KINDA A GOOD-NEWS, BAD-NEWS SITUATION.
NED? AS IN "NANCY AND NED?"
NED, YOUR BOYFRIEND, NED?
EX-BOYFRIEND, SINCE HE TOOK UP WITH A CLASSMATE NAMED DEIDRE.
MISUNDER-STANDINGS, HURT FEELINGS, LONG STORY.
WELL, SHORT STORY, GOOD NEWS IS, NED AND DEIDRE ARE HISTORY.
BAD NEWS IS...

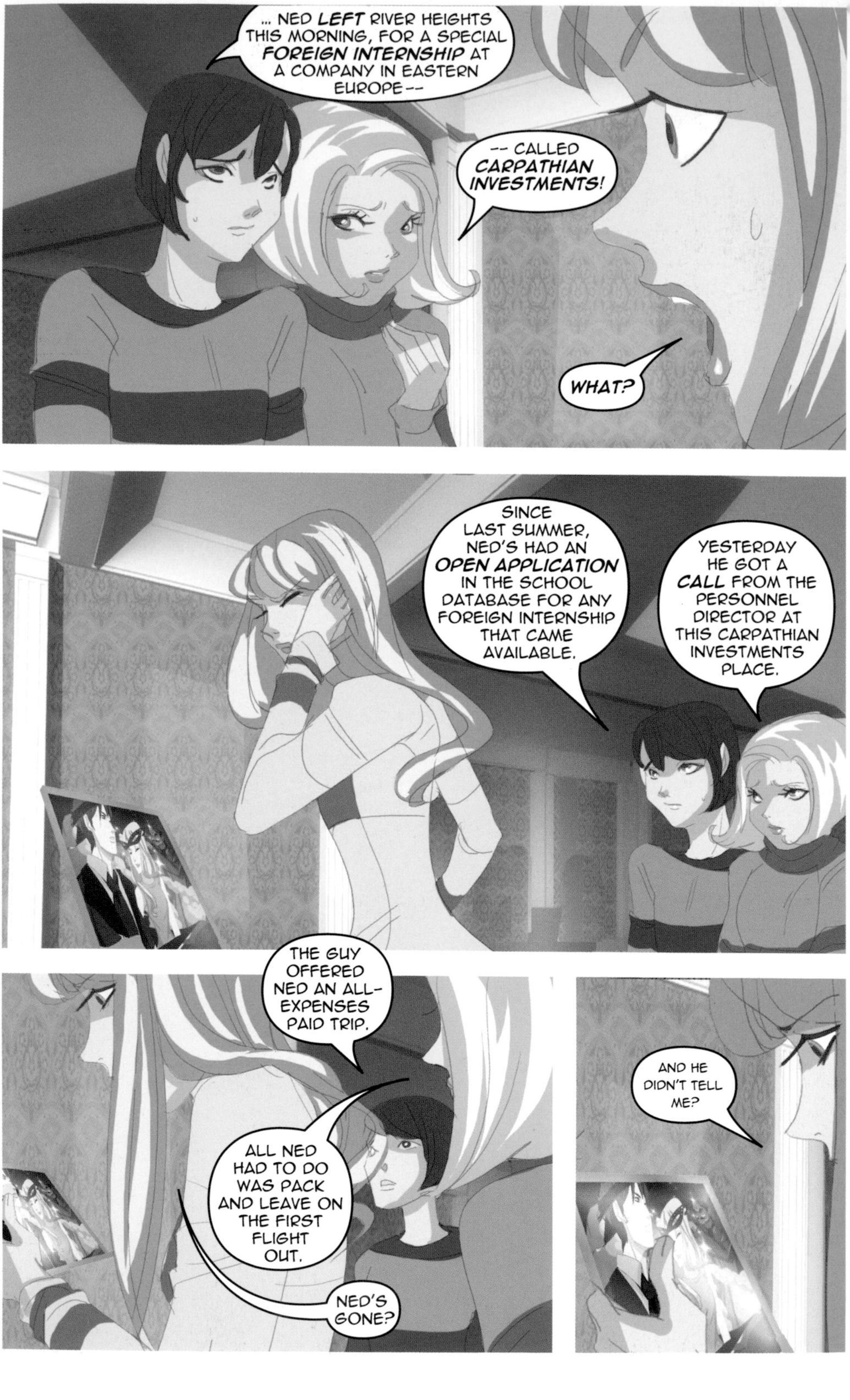
... NED **LEFT** RIVER HEIGHTS THIS MORNING, FOR A SPECIAL **FOREIGN INTERNSHIP** AT A COMPANY IN EASTERN EUROPE--
-- CALLED **CARPATHIAN INVESTMENTS!**
WHAT?
SINCE LAST SUMMER, NED'S HAD AN **OPEN APPLICATION** IN THE SCHOOL DATABASE FOR ANY FOREIGN INTERNSHIP THAT CAME AVAILABLE.
YESTERDAY HE GOT A **CALL** FROM THE PERSONNEL DIRECTOR AT THIS CARPATHIAN INVESTMENTS PLACE.
THE GUY OFFERED NED AN ALL-EXPENSES PAID TRIP.
ALL NED HAD TO DO WAS PACK AND LEAVE ON THE FIRST FLIGHT OUT.
NED'S GONE?
AND HE DIDN'T TELL ME?

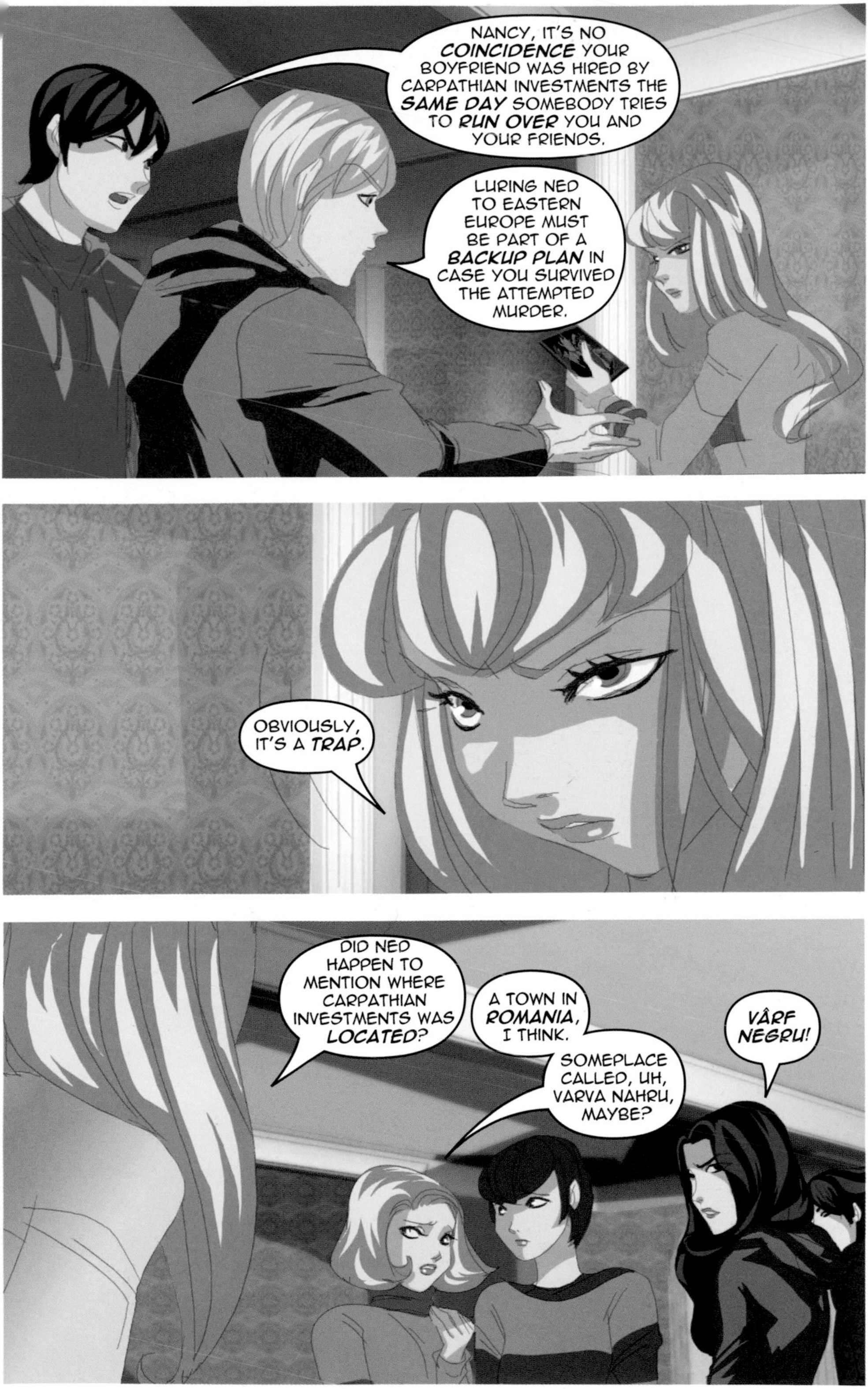
NANCY, IT'S NO COINCIDENCE YOUR BOYFRIEND WAS HIRED BY CARPATHIAN INVESTMENTS THE SAME DAY SOMEBODY TRIES TO RUN OVER YOU AND YOUR FRIENDS.
LURING NED TO EASTERN EUROPE MUST BE PART OF A BACKUP PLAN IN CASE YOU SURVIVED THE ATTEMPTED MURDER.
OBVIOUSLY, IT'S A TRAP.
DID NED HAPPEN TO MENTION WHERE CARPATHIAN INVESTMENTS WAS LOCATED?
A TOWN IN ROMANIA, I THINK.
SOMEPLACE CALLED, UH, VARVA NAHRU, MAYBE?
VÂRF NEGRU!

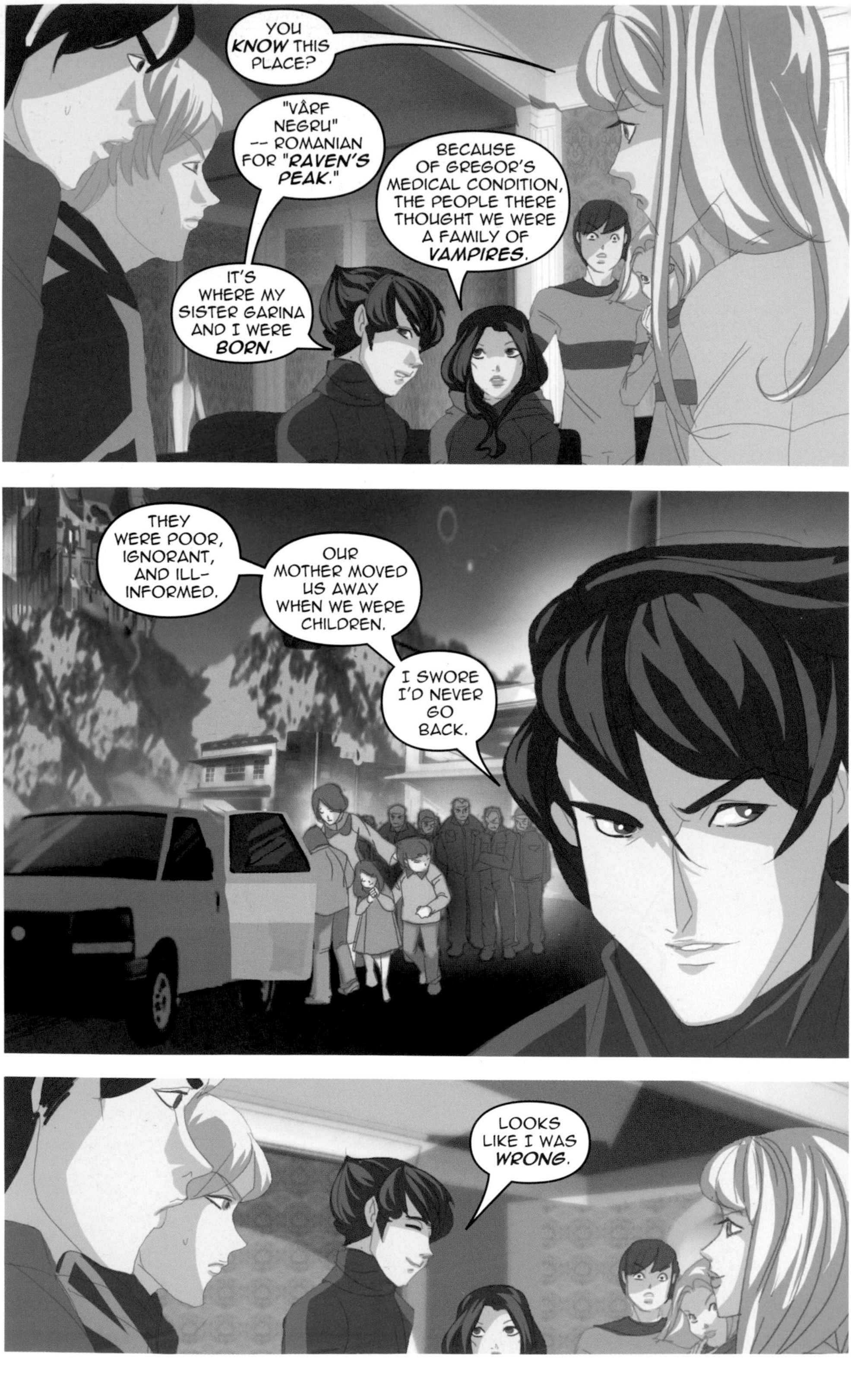
YOU KNOW THIS PLACE?
"VÂRF NEGRU" -- ROMANIAN FOR "RAVEN'S PEAK."
IT'S WHERE MY SISTER GARINA AND I WERE BORN.
BECAUSE OF GREGOR'S MEDICAL CONDITION, THE PEOPLE THERE THOUGHT WE WERE A FAMILY OF VAMPIRES.
THEY WERE POOR, IGNORANT, AND ILL-INFORMED.
OUR MOTHER MOVED US AWAY WHEN WE WERE CHILDREN.
I SWORE I'D NEVER GO BACK.
LOOKS LIKE I WAS WRONG.

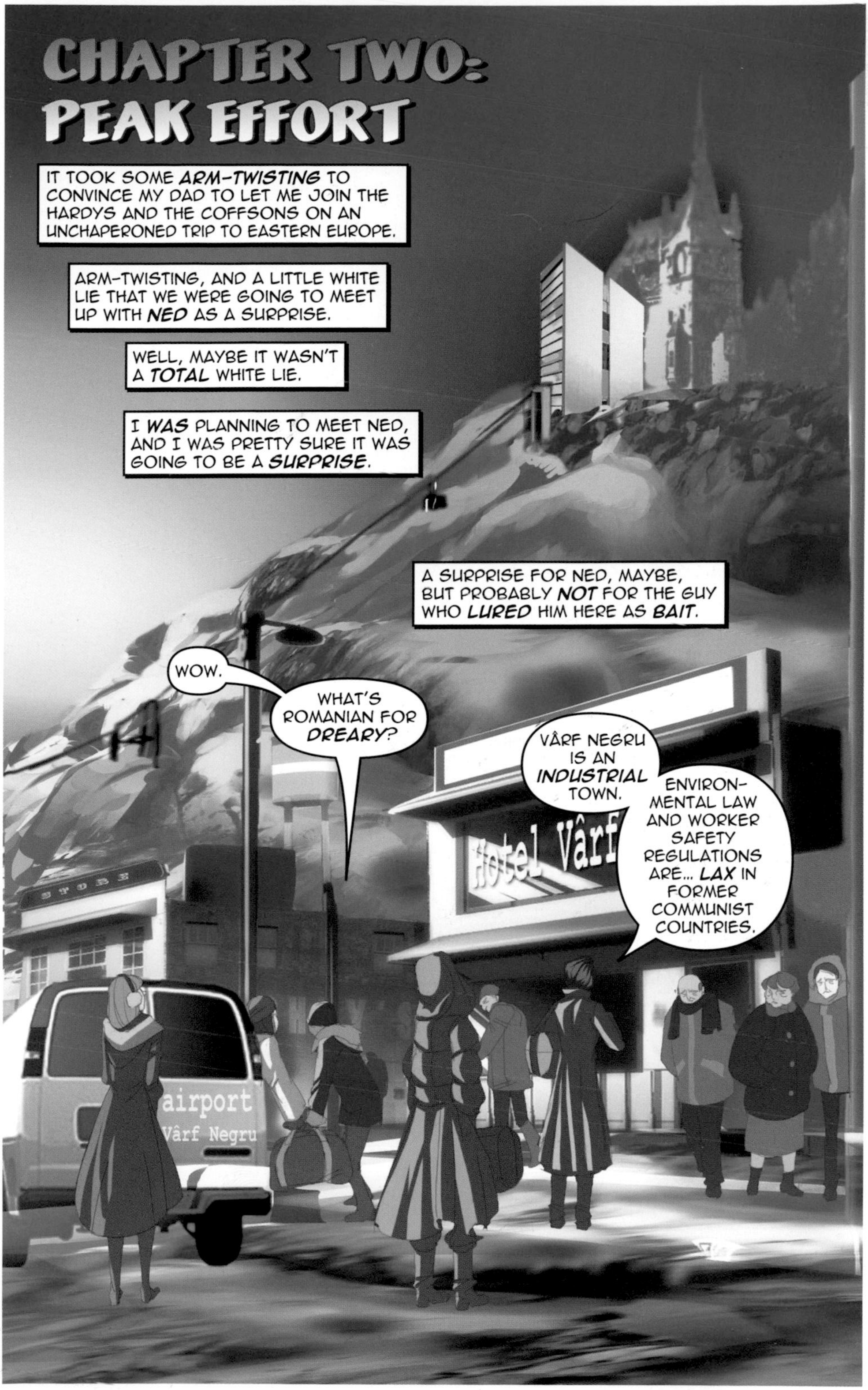
CHAPTER TWO: PEAK EFFORT
IT TOOK SOME ARM-TWISTING TO CONVINCE MY DAD TO LET ME JOIN THE HARDYS AND THE COFFSONS ON AN UNCHAPERONED TRIP TO EASTERN EUROPE.
ARM-TWISTING, AND A LITTLE WHITE LIE THAT WE WERE GOING TO MEET UP WITH NED AS A SURPRISE.
WELL, MAYBE IT WASN'T A TOTAL WHITE LIE.
I WAS PLANNING TO MEET NED, AND I WAS PRETTY SURE IT WAS GOING TO BE A SURPRISE.
A SURPRISE FOR NED, MAYBE, BUT PROBABLY NOT FOR THE GUY WHO LURED HIM HERE AS BAIT.
WOW.
WHAT'S ROMANIAN FOR DREARY?
VÂRF NEGRU IS AN INDUSTRIAL TOWN.
ENVIRONMENTAL LAW AND WORKER SAFETY REGULATIONS ARE... LAX IN FORMER COMMUNIST COUNTRIES.
STORE
Hotel Vârf
airport
Vârf Negru

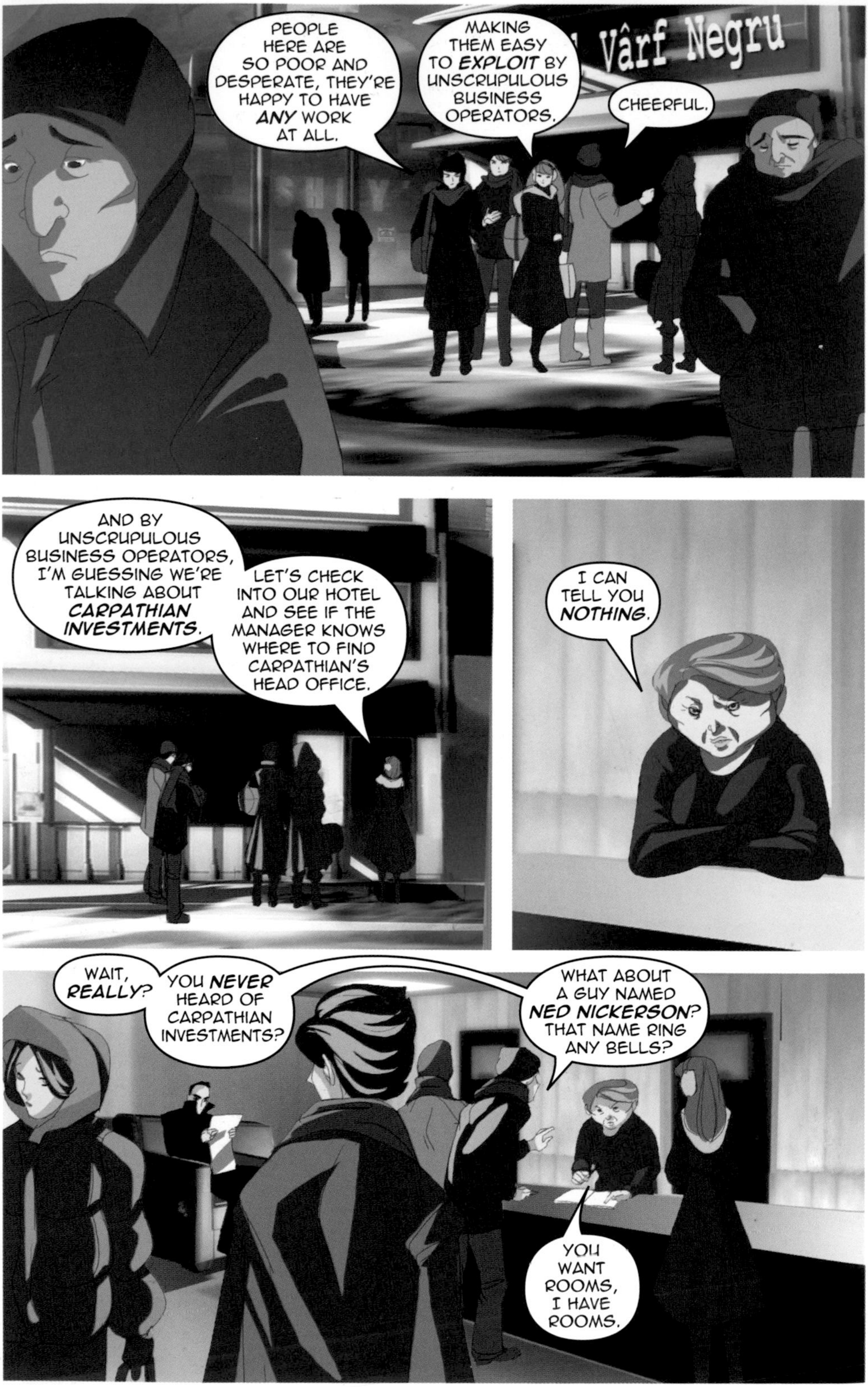
Vârf Negru
PEOPLE HERE ARE SO POOR AND DESPERATE, THEY'RE HAPPY TO HAVE ANY WORK AT ALL.
MAKING THEM EASY TO EXPLOIT BY UNSCRUPULOUS BUSINESS OPERATORS.
CHEERFUL.
AND BY UNSCRUPULOUS BUSINESS OPERATORS, I'M GUESSING WE'RE TALKING ABOUT CARPATHIAN INVESTMENTS.
LET'S CHECK INTO OUR HOTEL AND SEE IF THE MANAGER KNOWS WHERE TO FIND CARPATHIAN'S HEAD OFFICE.
I CAN TELL YOU NOTHING.
WAIT, REALLY?
YOU NEVER HEARD OF CARPATHIAN INVESTMENTS?
WHAT ABOUT A GUY NAMED NED NICKERSON? THAT NAME RING ANY BELLS?
YOU WANT ROOMS, I HAVE ROOMS.

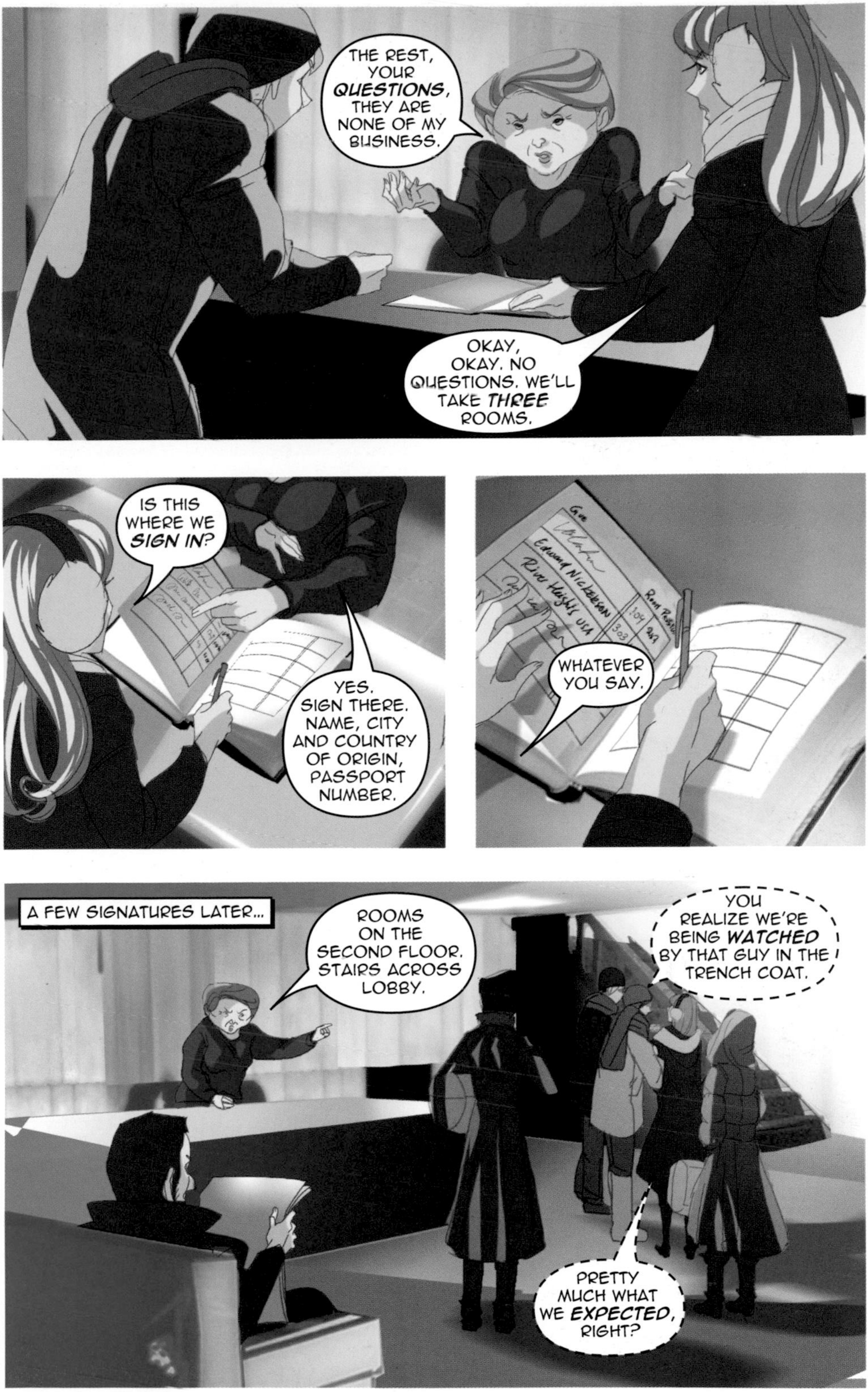

THE REST, YOUR *QUESTIONS*, THEY ARE NONE OF MY BUSINESS.
OKAY, OKAY. NO QUESTIONS. WE'LL TAKE *THREE* ROOMS.
IS THIS WHERE WE *SIGN IN*?
YES. SIGN THERE. NAME, CITY AND COUNTRY OF ORIGIN, PASSPORT NUMBER.
Edward Nickerson
River Heights USA
WHATEVER YOU SAY.
A FEW SIGNATURES LATER...
ROOMS ON THE SECOND FLOOR. STAIRS ACROSS LOBBY.
YOU REALIZE WE'RE BEING *WATCHED* BY THAT GUY IN THE TRENCH COAT.
PRETTY MUCH WHAT WE *EXPECTED*, RIGHT?

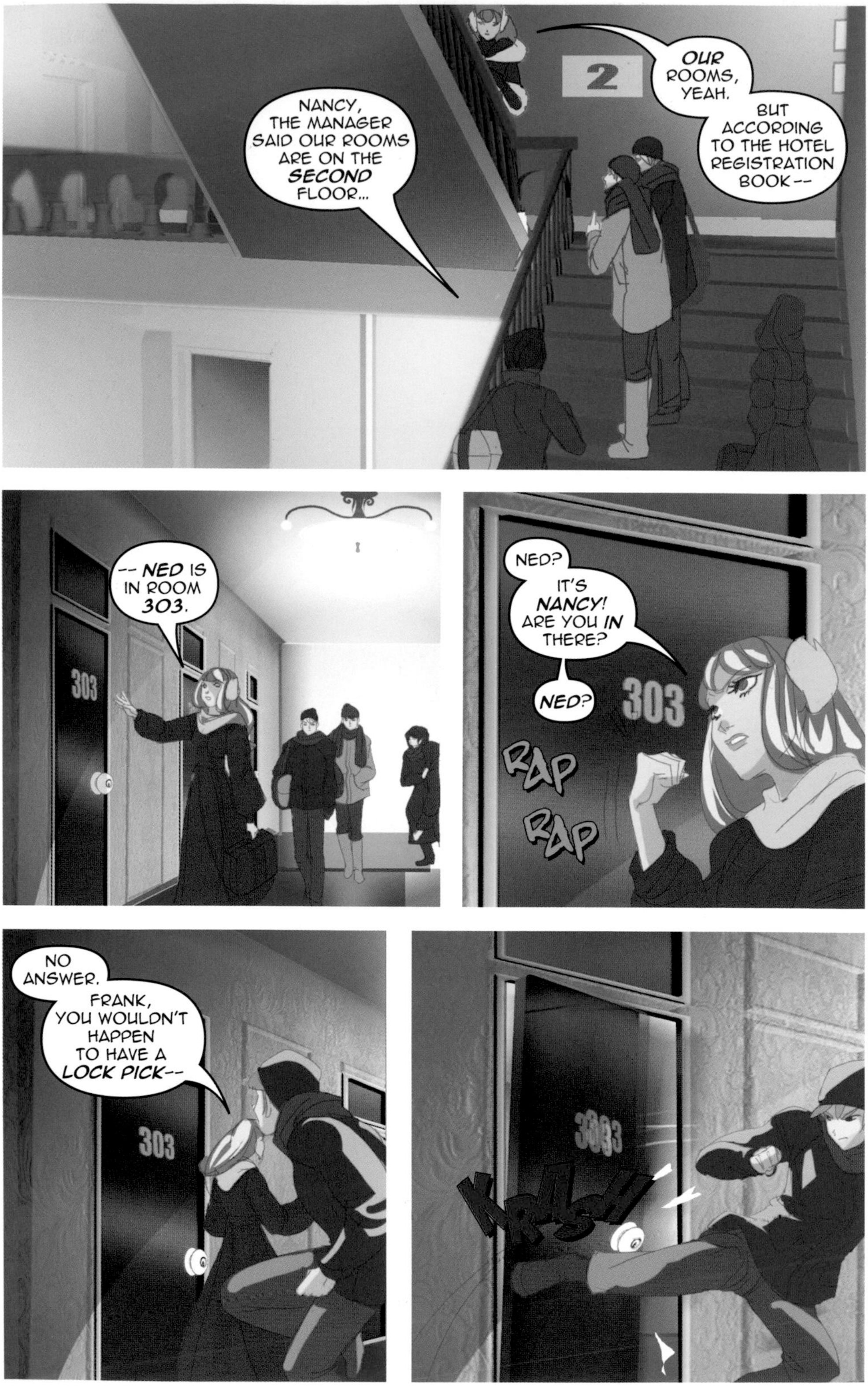
NANCY, THE MANAGER SAID OUR ROOMS ARE ON THE SECOND FLOOR...
OUR ROOMS, YEAH.
BUT ACCORDING TO THE HOTEL REGISTRATION BOOK--
2
--NED IS IN ROOM 303.
303
NED?
IT'S NANCY! ARE YOU IN THERE?
NED?
303
RAP
RAP
NO ANSWER.
FRANK, YOU WOULDN'T HAPPEN TO HAVE A LOCK PICK--
303
KRASH!

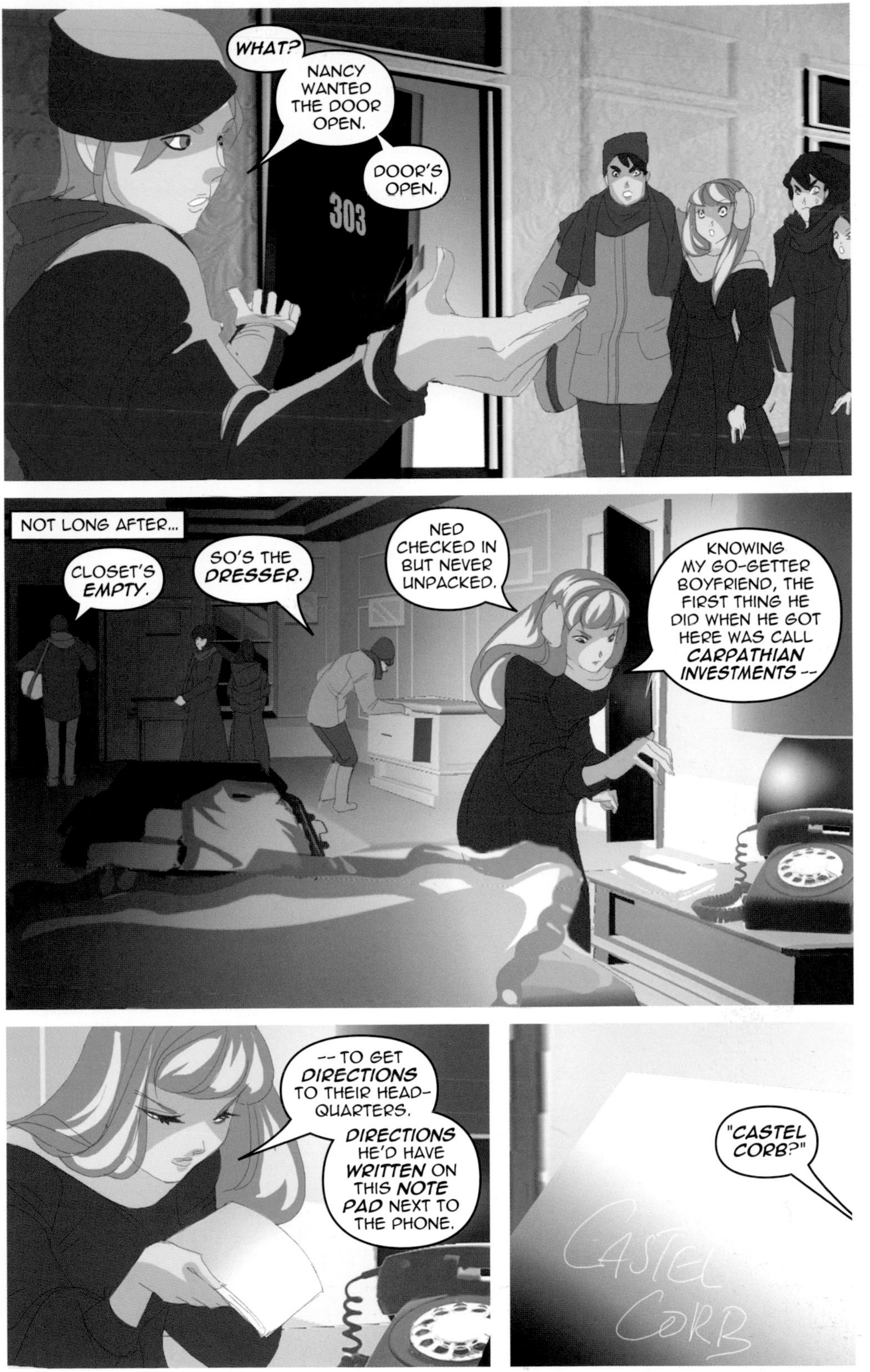
WHAT?
NANCY WANTED THE DOOR OPEN.
DOOR'S OPEN.
303
NOT LONG AFTER...
CLOSET'S EMPTY.
SO'S THE DRESSER.
NED CHECKED IN BUT NEVER UNPACKED.
KNOWING MY GO-GETTER BOYFRIEND, THE FIRST THING HE DID WHEN HE GOT HERE WAS CALL CARPATHIAN INVESTMENTS --
-- TO GET DIRECTIONS TO THEIR HEAD-QUARTERS.
DIRECTIONS HE'D HAVE WRITTEN ON THIS NOTE PAD NEXT TO THE PHONE.
"CASTEL CORB?"
CASTEL CORB

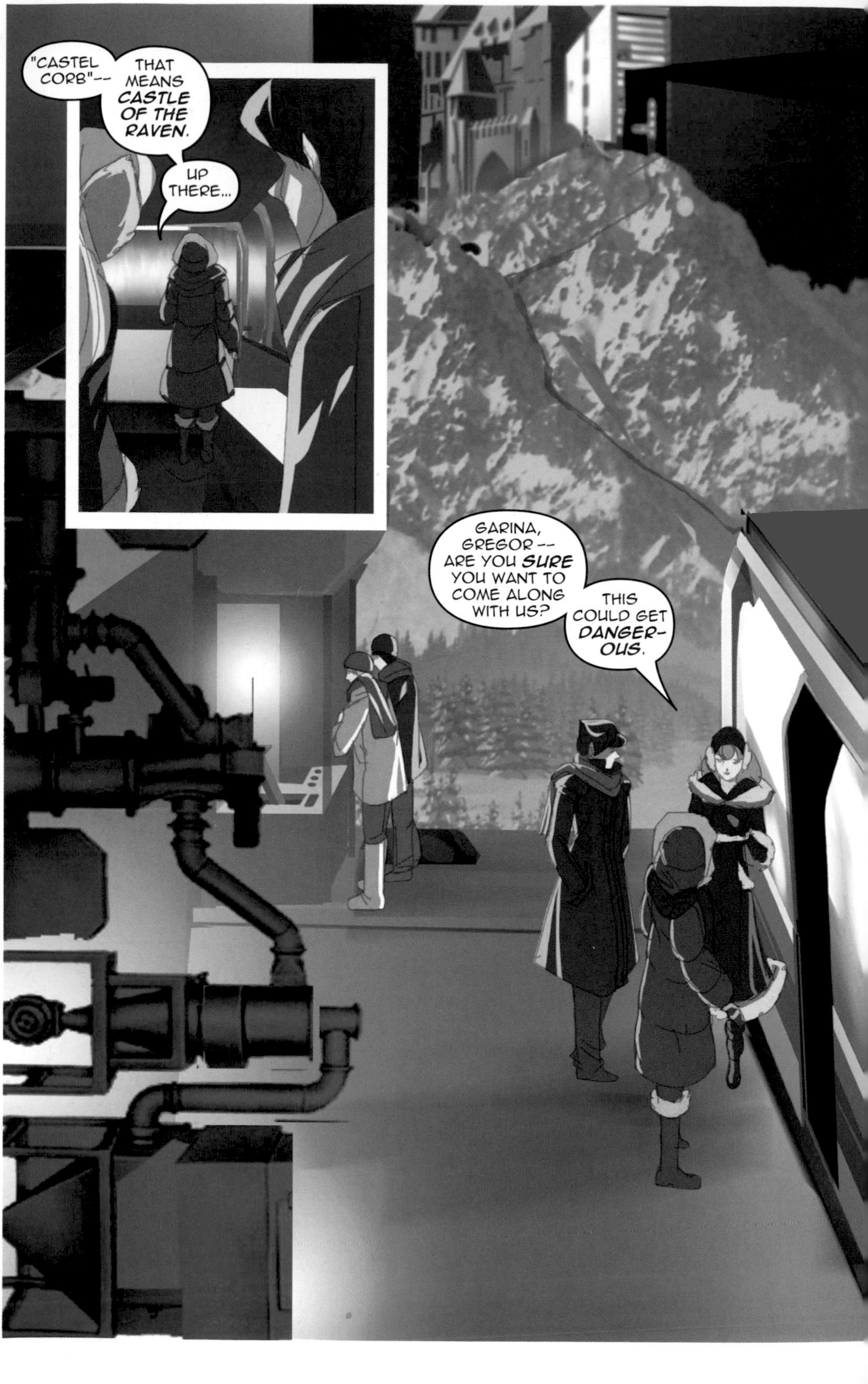
"CASTEL CORB"--
THAT MEANS CASTLE OF THE RAVEN.
UP THERE...
GARINA, GREGOR -- ARE YOU SURE YOU WANT TO COME ALONG WITH US?
THIS COULD GET DANGER-OUS.

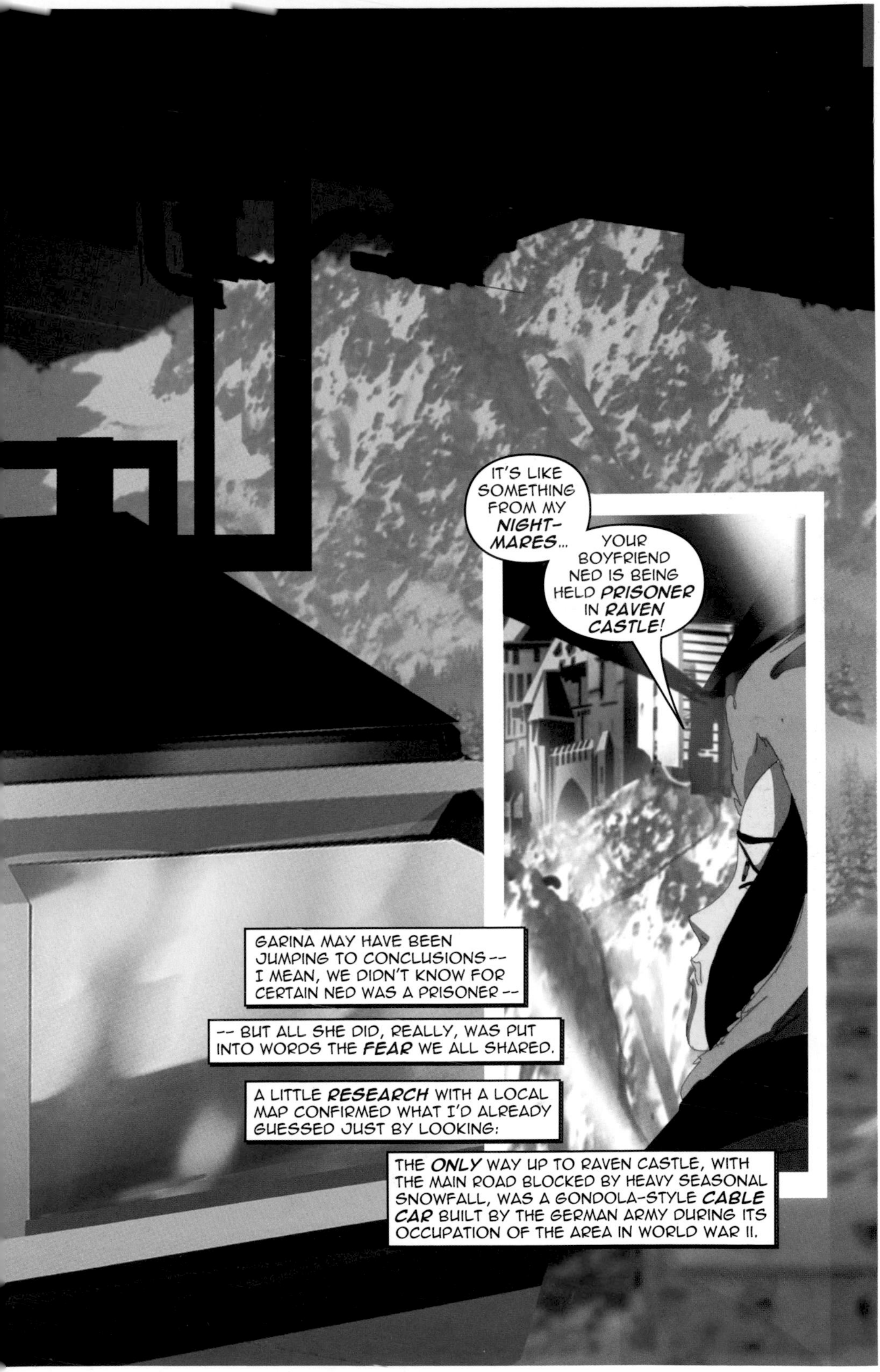
IT'S LIKE SOMETHING FROM MY NIGHT-MARES...
YOUR BOYFRIEND NED IS BEING HELD PRISONER IN RAVEN CASTLE!
GARINA MAY HAVE BEEN JUMPING TO CONCLUSIONS -- I MEAN, WE DIDN'T KNOW FOR CERTAIN NED WAS A PRISONER --
-- BUT ALL SHE DID, REALLY, WAS PUT INTO WORDS THE FEAR WE ALL SHARED.
A LITTLE RESEARCH WITH A LOCAL MAP CONFIRMED WHAT I'D ALREADY GUESSED JUST BY LOOKING:
THE ONLY WAY UP TO RAVEN CASTLE, WITH THE MAIN ROAD BLOCKED BY HEAVY SEASONAL SNOWFALL, WAS A GONDOLA-STYLE CABLE CAR BUILT BY THE GERMAN ARMY DURING ITS OCCUPATION OF THE AREA IN WORLD WAR II.

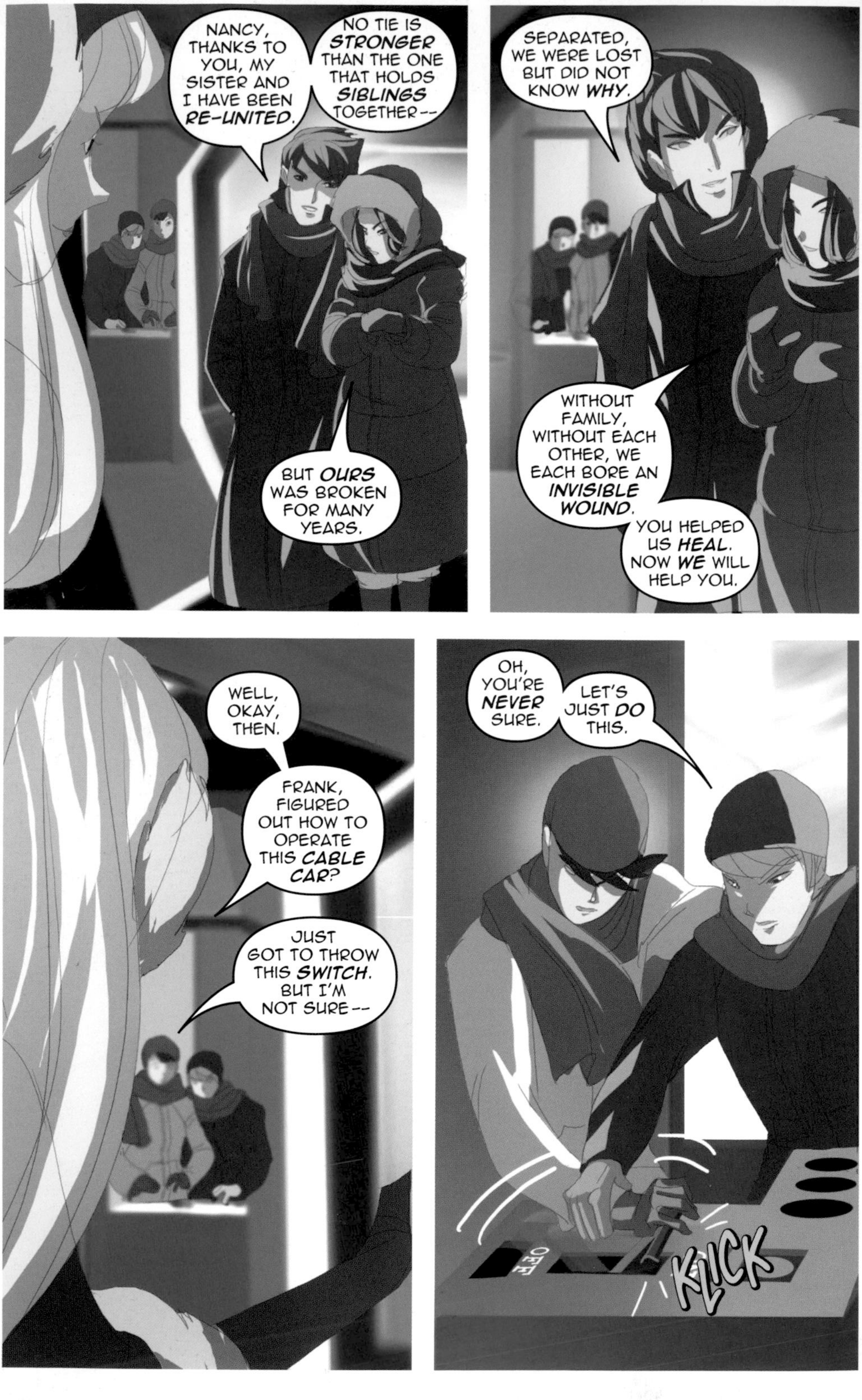
NANCY, THANKS TO YOU, MY SISTER AND I HAVE BEEN RE-UNITED.
NO TIE IS STRONGER THAN THE ONE THAT HOLDS SIBLINGS TOGETHER--
BUT OURS WAS BROKEN FOR MANY YEARS.
SEPARATED, WE WERE LOST BUT DID NOT KNOW WHY.
WITHOUT FAMILY, WITHOUT EACH OTHER, WE EACH BORE AN INVISIBLE WOUND.
YOU HELPED US HEAL. NOW WE WILL HELP YOU.
WELL, OKAY, THEN.
FRANK, FIGURED OUT HOW TO OPERATE THIS CABLE CAR?
JUST GOT TO THROW THIS SWITCH. BUT I'M NOT SURE--
OH, YOU'RE NEVER SURE.
LET'S JUST DO THIS.
OFF
KLICK

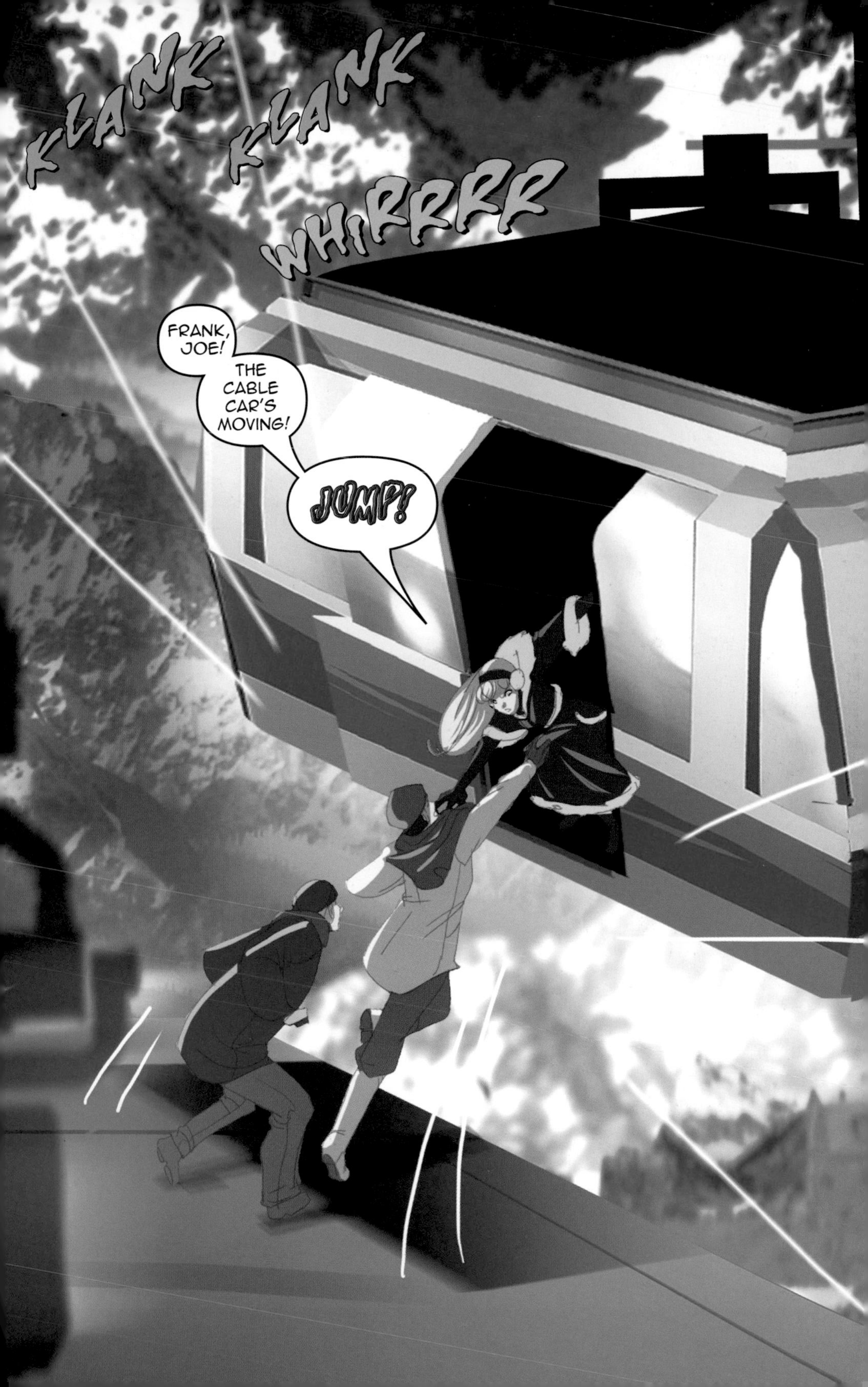
KLANK KLANK
WHIRRRR
FRANK, JOE!
THE CABLE CAR'S MOVING!
JUMP!

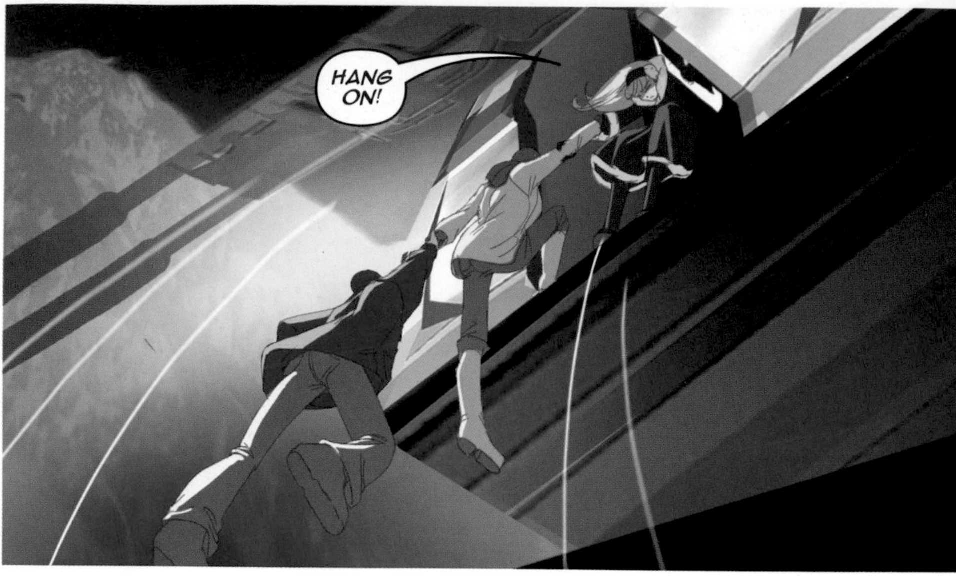
HANG ON!

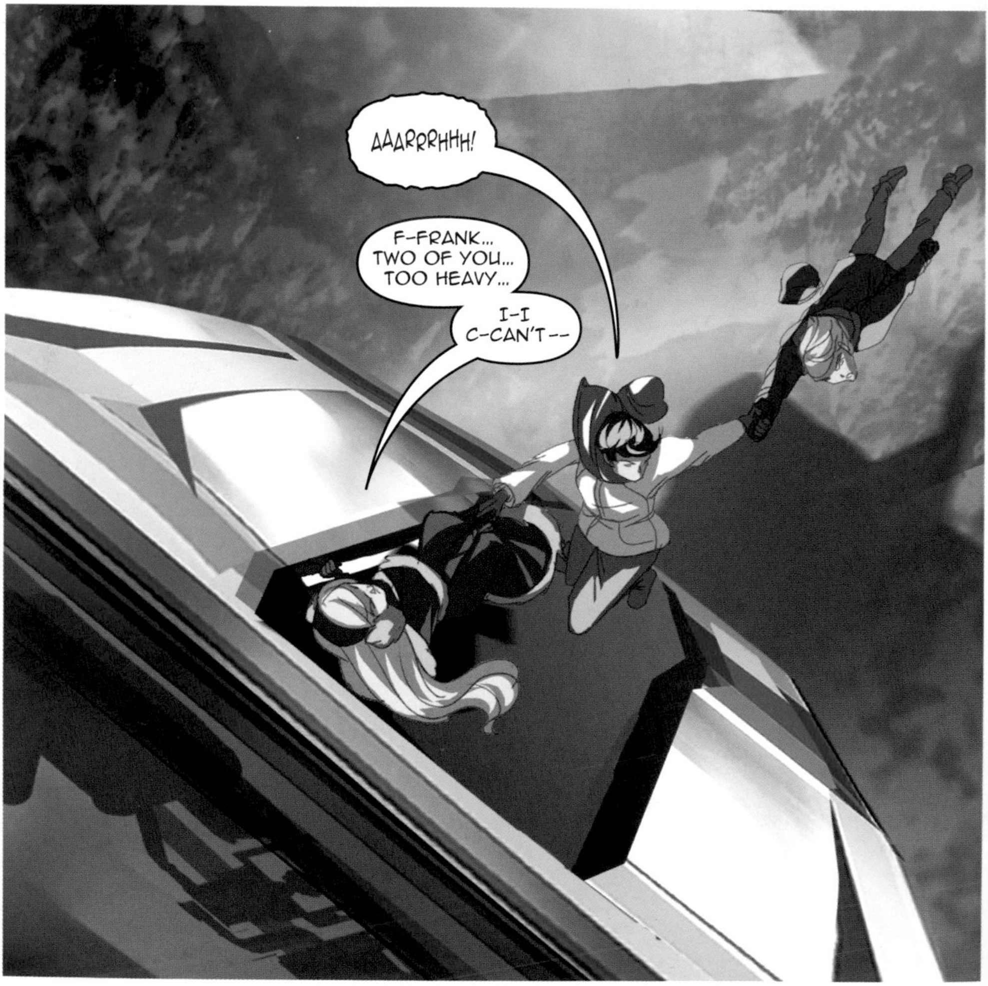
AAARRRHHH!
F-FRANK... TWO OF YOU... TOO HEAVY...
I-I C-CAN'T --

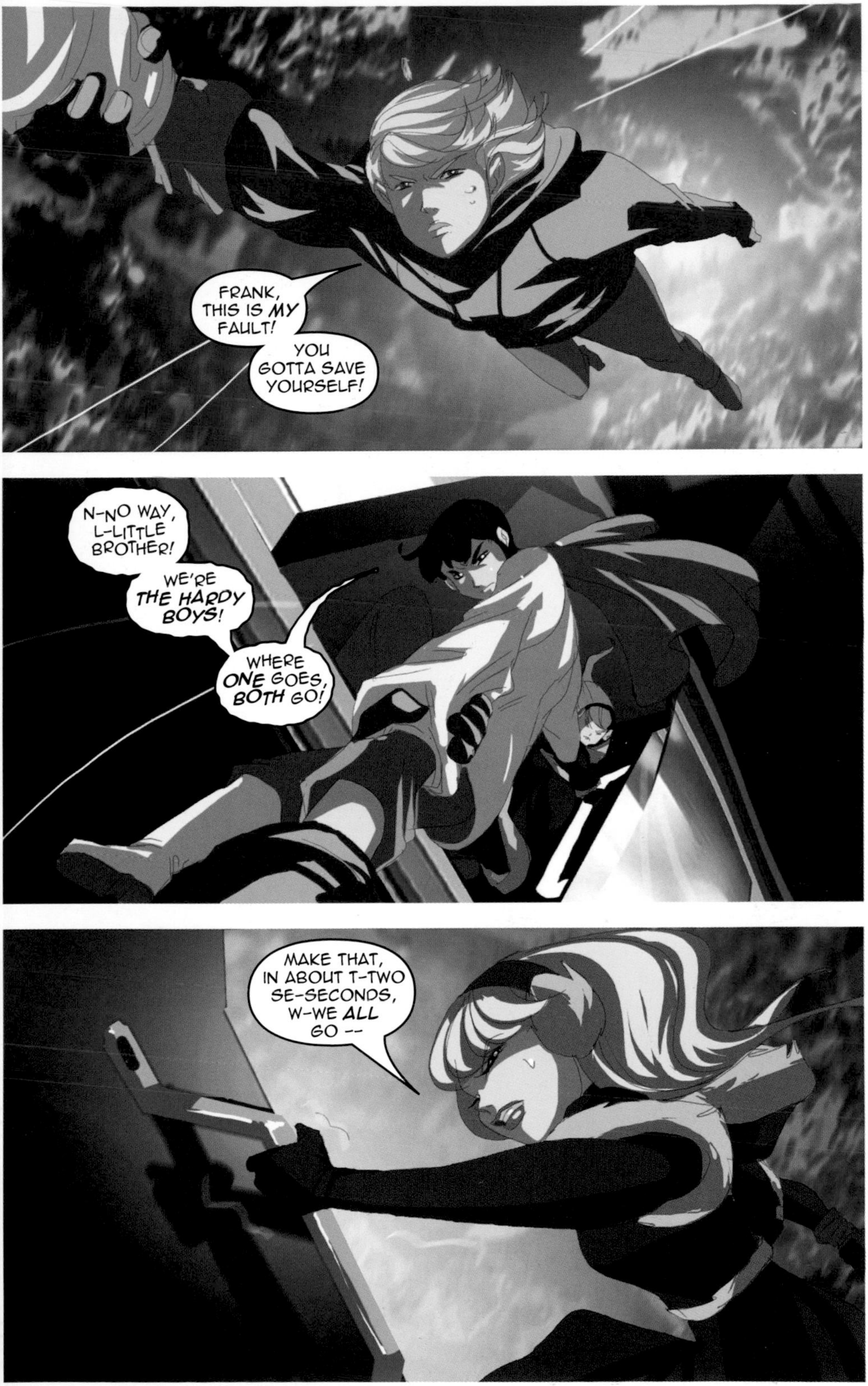
FRANK, THIS IS MY FAULT!
YOU GOTTA SAVE YOURSELF!
N-NO WAY, L-LITTLE BROTHER!
WE'RE THE HARDY BOYS!
WHERE ONE GOES, BOTH GO!
MAKE THAT, IN ABOUT T-TWO SE-SECONDS, W-WE ALL GO --

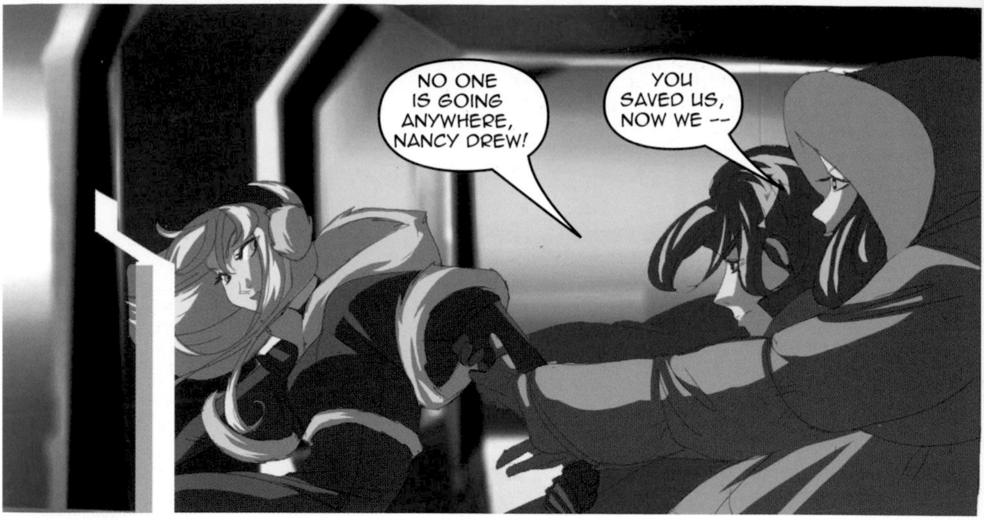
NO ONE IS GOING ANYWHERE, NANCY DREW!
YOU SAVED US, NOW WE --

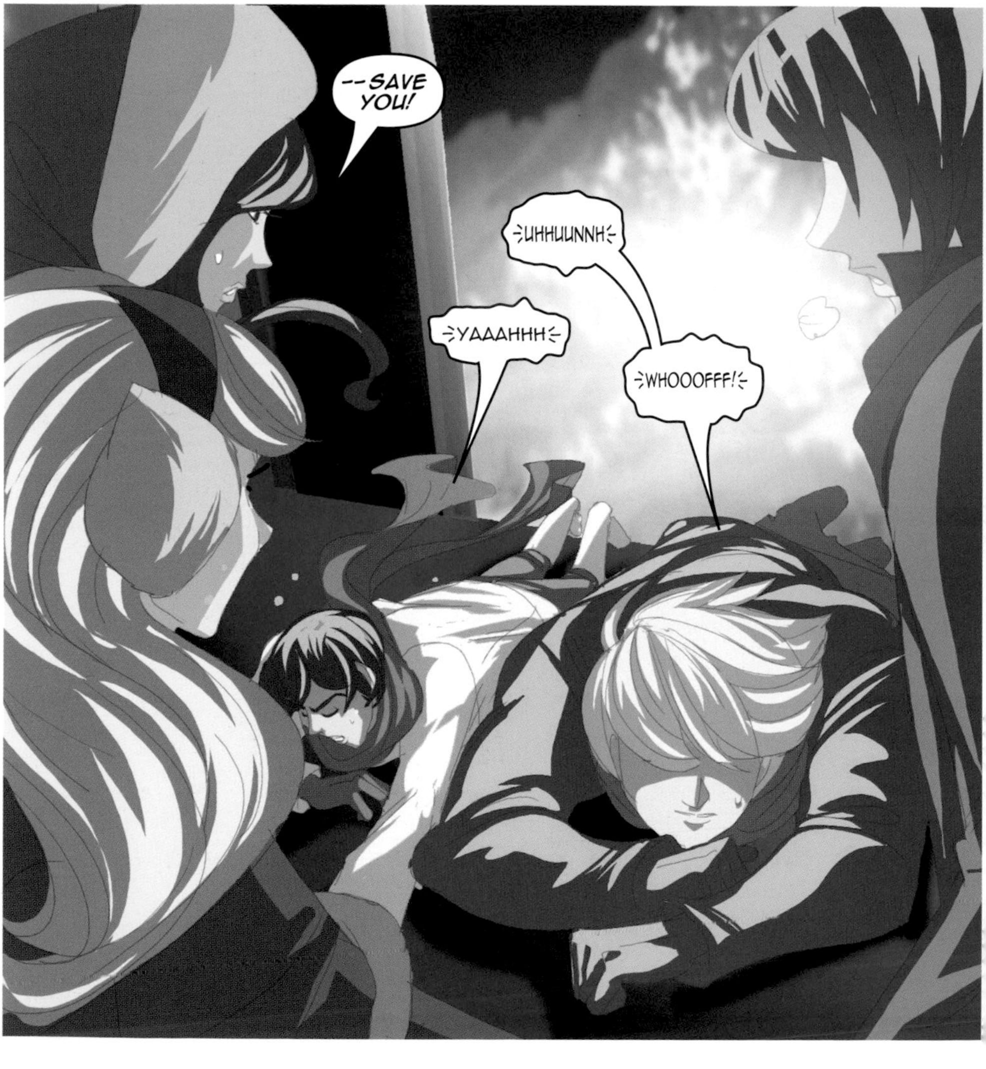
--SAVE YOU!
UHHUUNNH
YAAAHHH
WHOOOFFF!

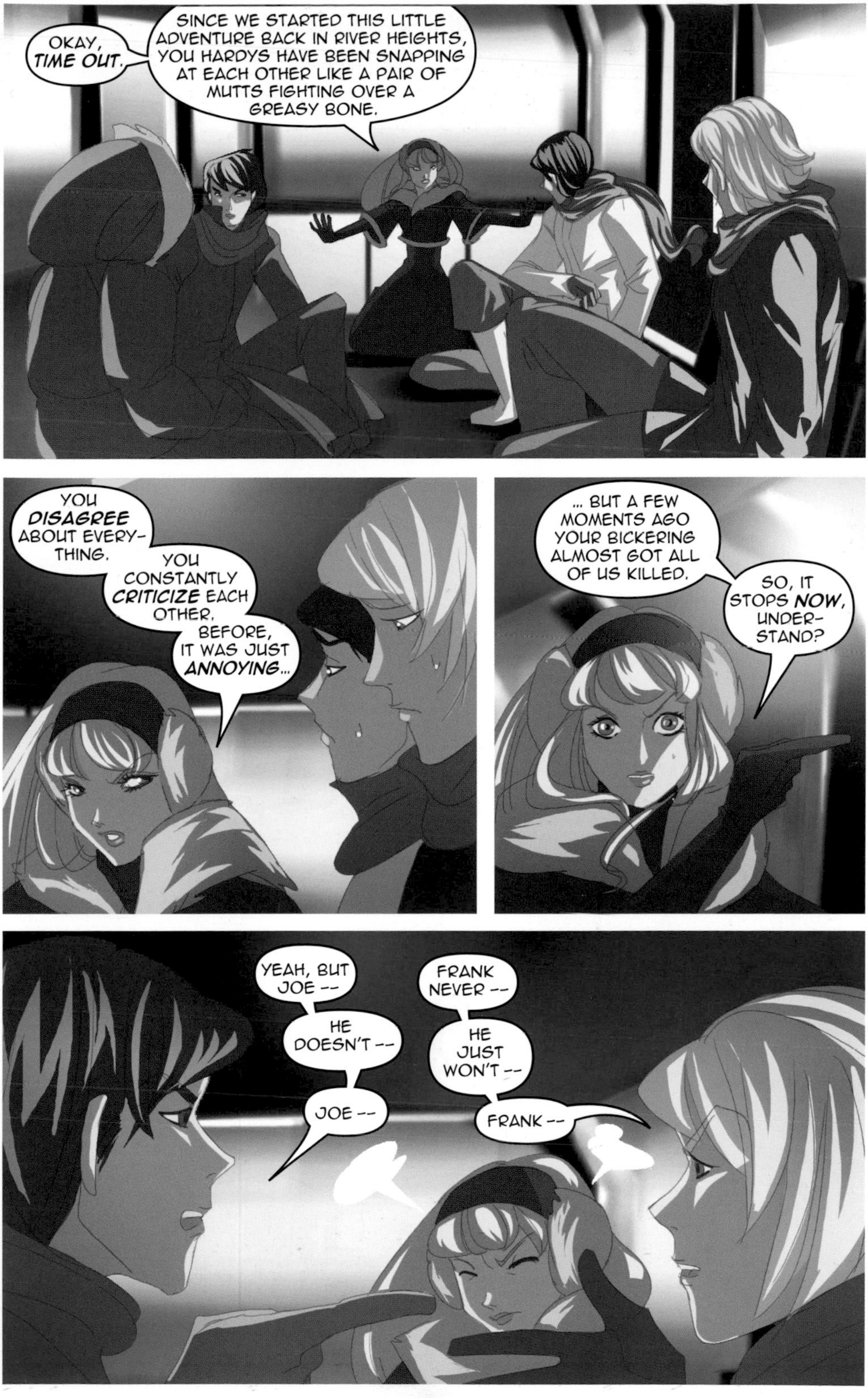
OKAY, TIME OUT.
SINCE WE STARTED THIS LITTLE ADVENTURE BACK IN RIVER HEIGHTS, YOU HARDYS HAVE BEEN SNAPPING AT EACH OTHER LIKE A PAIR OF MUTTS FIGHTING OVER A GREASY BONE.
YOU DISAGREE ABOUT EVERY-THING.
YOU CONSTANTLY CRITICIZE EACH OTHER.
BEFORE, IT WAS JUST ANNOYING...
... BUT A FEW MOMENTS AGO YOUR BICKERING ALMOST GOT ALL OF US KILLED.
SO, IT STOPS NOW, UNDER-STAND?
YEAH, BUT JOE --
HE DOESN'T --
JOE --
FRANK NEVER --
HE JUST WON'T --
FRANK --

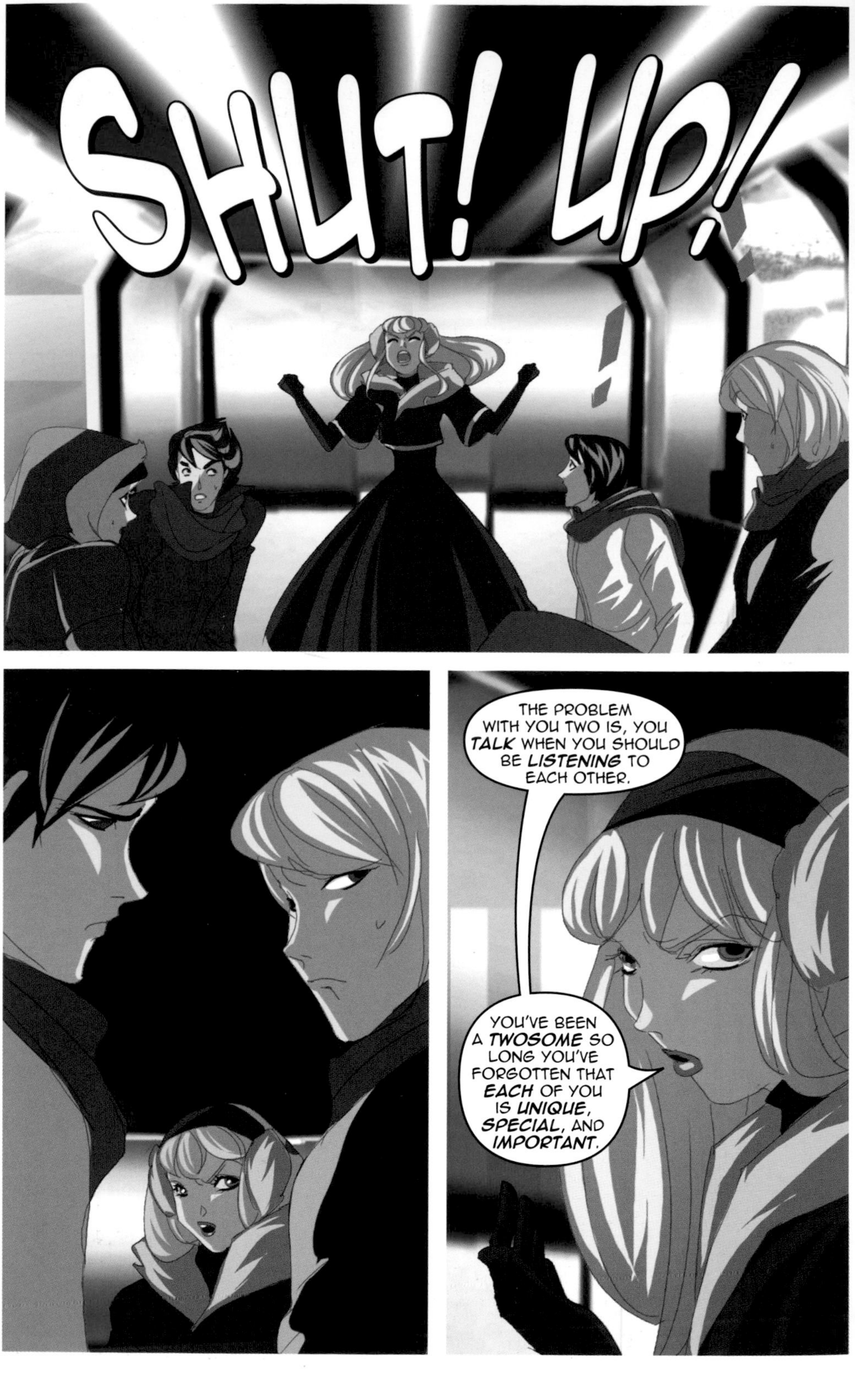
SHUT! UP!
THE PROBLEM WITH YOU TWO IS, YOU *TALK* WHEN YOU SHOULD BE *LISTENING* TO EACH OTHER.
YOU'VE BEEN A *TWOSOME* SO LONG YOU'VE FORGOTTEN THAT *EACH* OF YOU IS *UNIQUE*, *SPECIAL*, AND *IMPORTANT*.

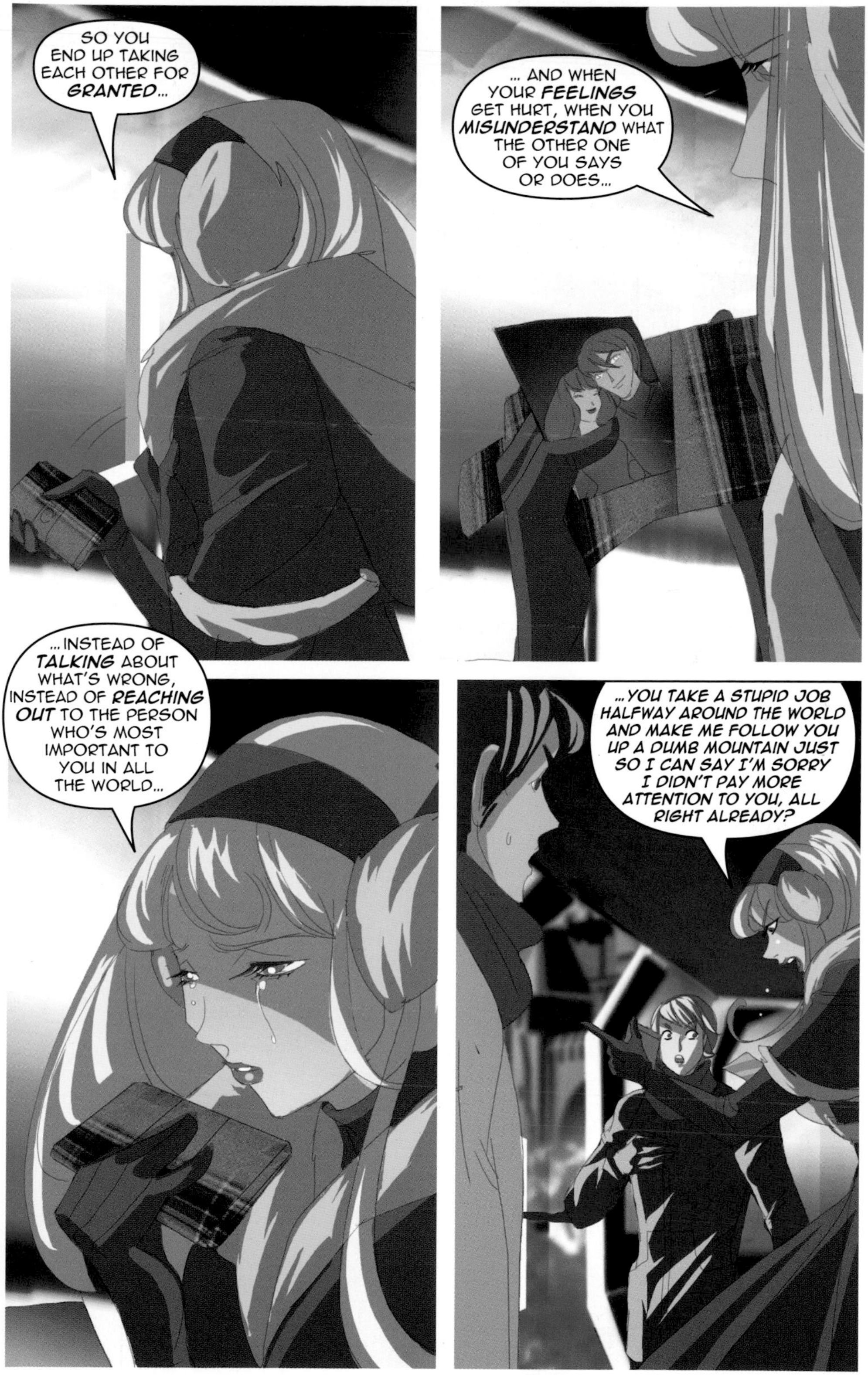
SO YOU END UP TAKING EACH OTHER FOR GRANTED...
... AND WHEN YOUR FEELINGS GET HURT, WHEN YOU MISUNDERSTAND WHAT THE OTHER ONE OF YOU SAYS OR DOES...
...INSTEAD OF TALKING ABOUT WHAT'S WRONG, INSTEAD OF REACHING OUT TO THE PERSON WHO'S MOST IMPORTANT TO YOU IN ALL THE WORLD...
...YOU TAKE A STUPID JOB HALFWAY AROUND THE WORLD AND MAKE ME FOLLOW YOU UP A DUMB MOUNTAIN JUST SO I CAN SAY I'M SORRY I DIDN'T PAY MORE ATTENTION TO YOU, ALL RIGHT ALREADY?

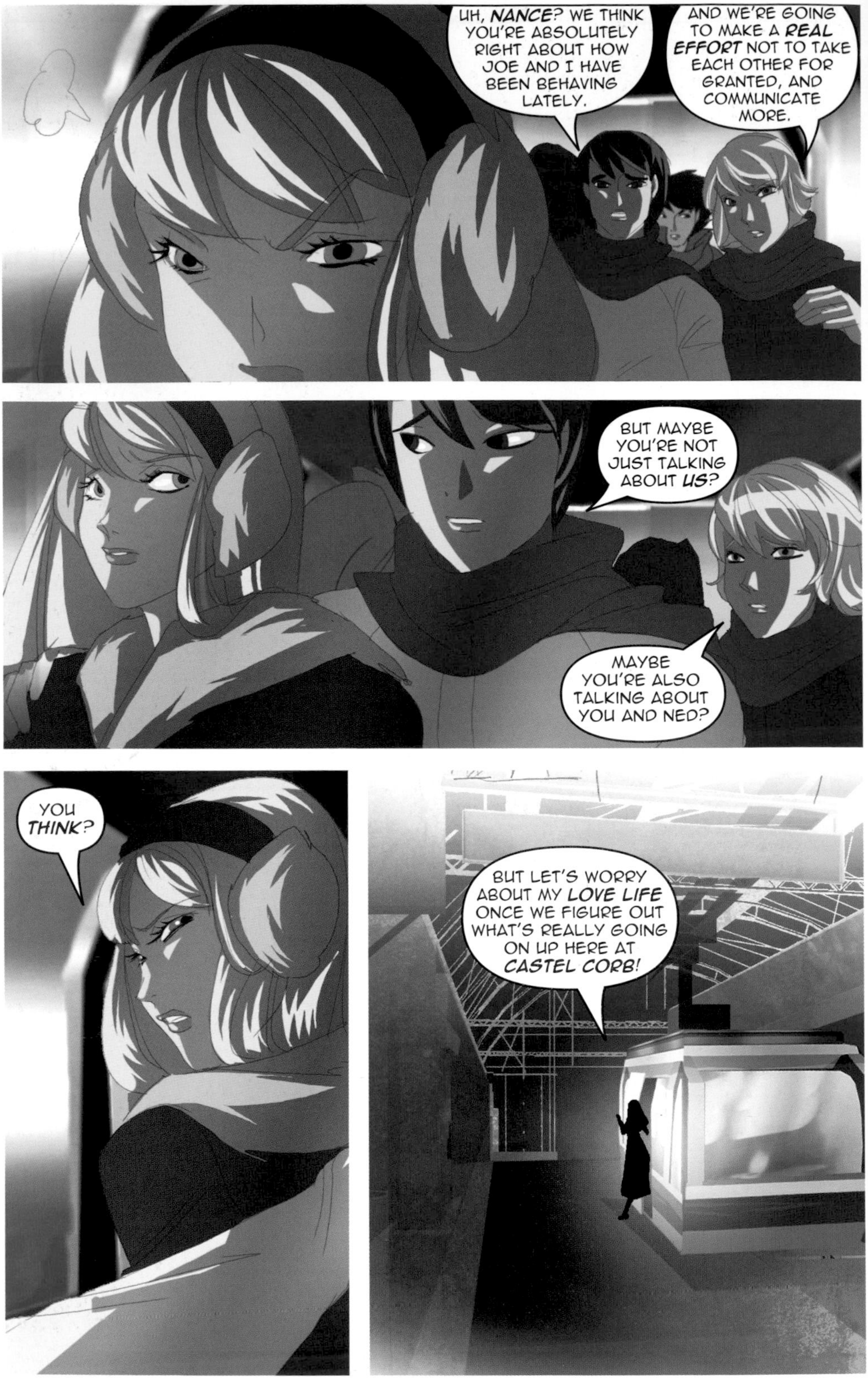
UH, NANCE? WE THINK YOU'RE ABSOLUTELY RIGHT ABOUT HOW JOE AND I HAVE BEEN BEHAVING LATELY.
AND WE'RE GOING TO MAKE A REAL EFFORT NOT TO TAKE EACH OTHER FOR GRANTED, AND COMMUNICATE MORE.
BUT MAYBE YOU'RE NOT JUST TALKING ABOUT US?
MAYBE YOU'RE ALSO TALKING ABOUT YOU AND NED?
YOU THINK?
BUT LET'S WORRY ABOUT MY LOVE LIFE ONCE WE FIGURE OUT WHAT'S REALLY GOING ON UP HERE AT CASTEL CORB!

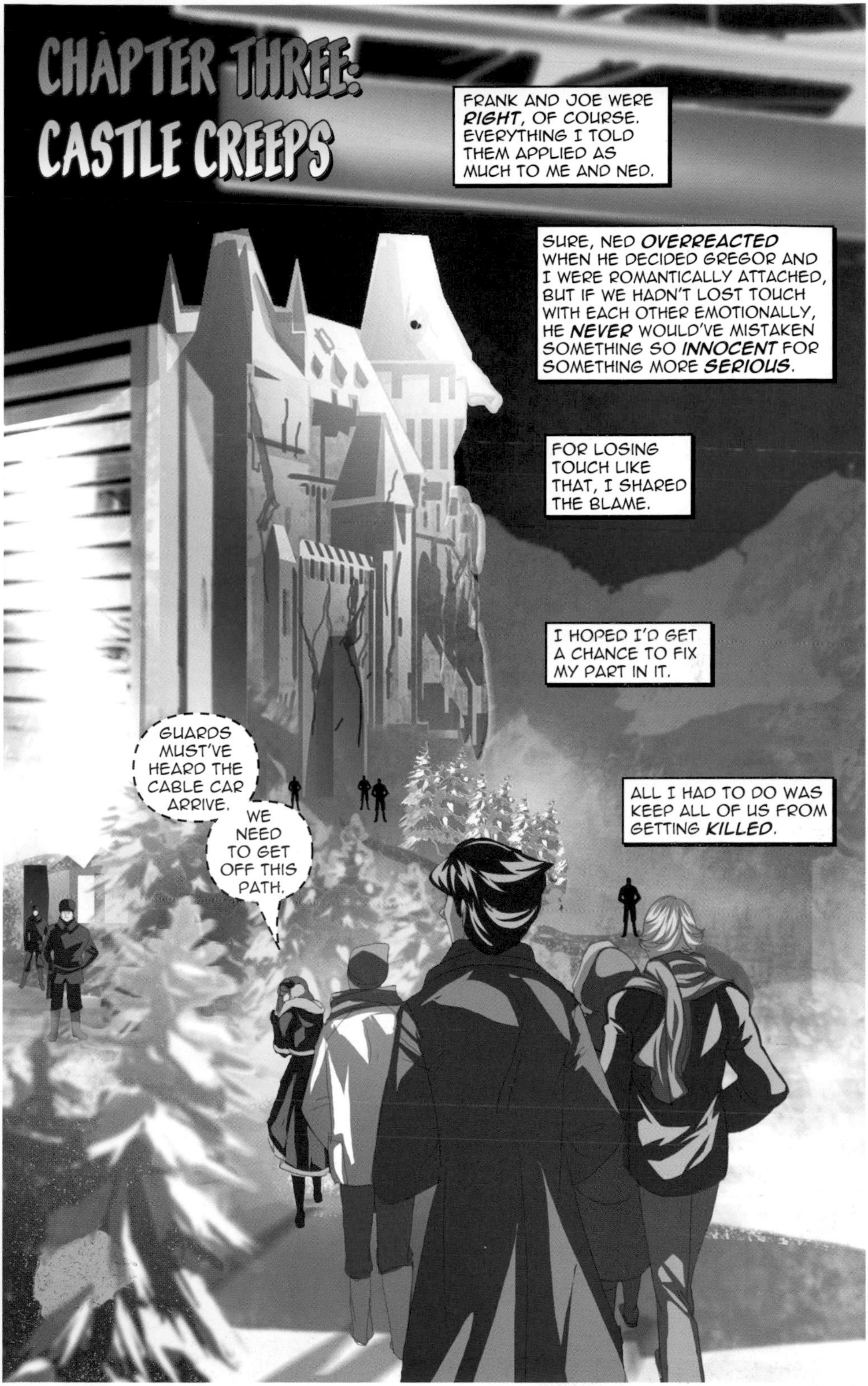
CHAPTER THREE: CASTLE CREEPS
FRANK AND JOE WERE RIGHT, OF COURSE. EVERYTHING I TOLD THEM APPLIED AS MUCH TO ME AND NED.
SURE, NED OVERREACTED WHEN HE DECIDED GREGOR AND I WERE ROMANTICALLY ATTACHED, BUT IF WE HADN'T LOST TOUCH WITH EACH OTHER EMOTIONALLY, HE NEVER WOULD'VE MISTAKEN SOMETHING SO INNOCENT FOR SOMETHING MORE SERIOUS.
FOR LOSING TOUCH LIKE THAT, I SHARED THE BLAME.
I HOPED I'D GET A CHANCE TO FIX MY PART IN IT.
GUARDS MUST'VE HEARD THE CABLE CAR ARRIVE.
WE NEED TO GET OFF THIS PATH.
ALL I HAD TO DO WAS KEEP ALL OF US FROM GETTING KILLED.

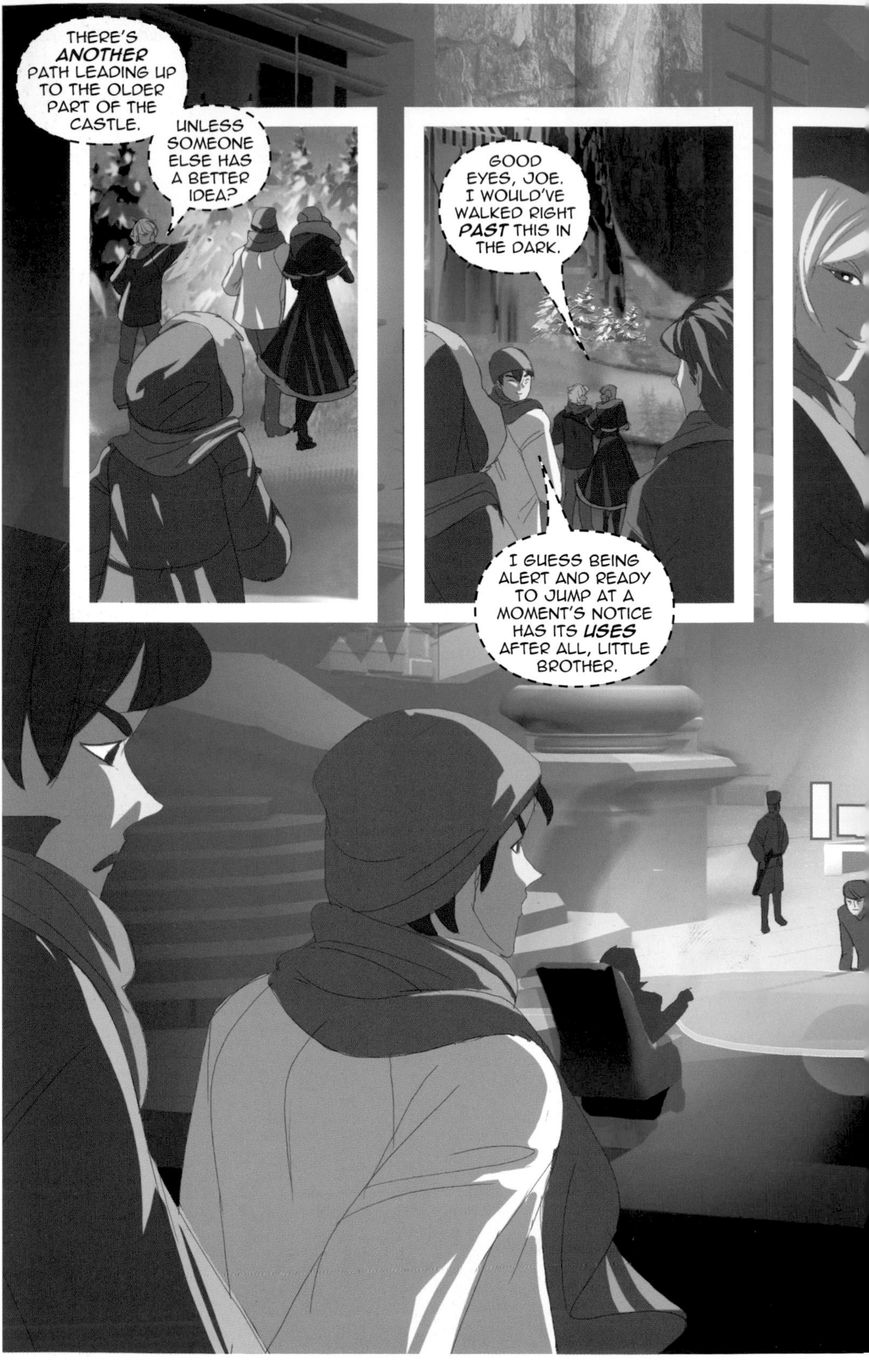

THERE'S ANOTHER PATH LEADING UP TO THE OLDER PART OF THE CASTLE.
UNLESS SOMEONE ELSE HAS A BETTER IDEA?
GOOD EYES, JOE. I WOULD'VE WALKED RIGHT PAST THIS IN THE DARK.
I GUESS BEING ALERT AND READY TO JUMP AT A MOMENT'S NOTICE HAS ITS USES AFTER ALL, LITTLE BROTHER.

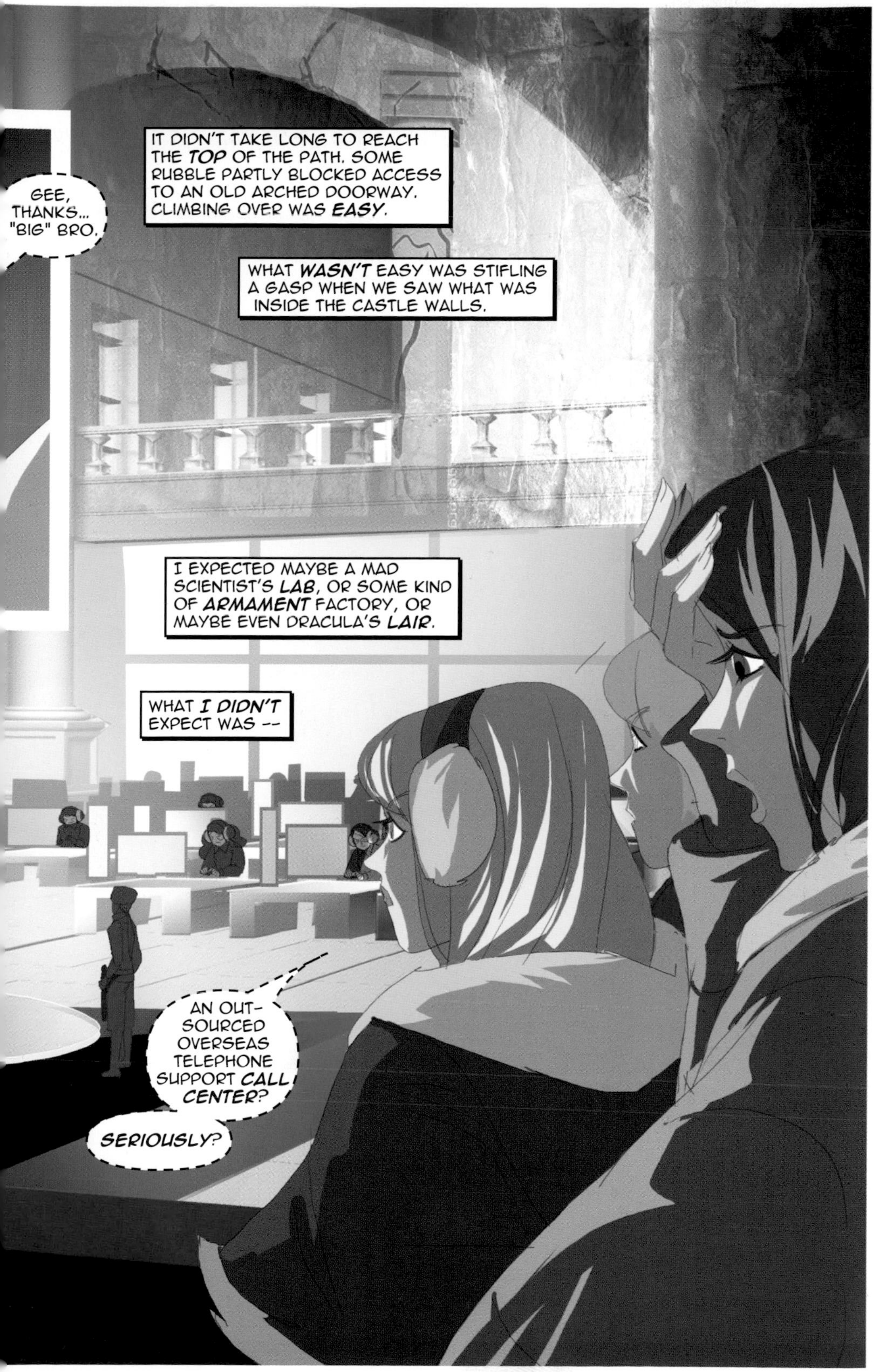
GEE, THANKS... "BIG" BRO.
IT DIDN'T TAKE LONG TO REACH THE TOP OF THE PATH. SOME RUBBLE PARTLY BLOCKED ACCESS TO AN OLD ARCHED DOORWAY. CLIMBING OVER WAS EASY.
WHAT WASN'T EASY WAS STIFLING A GASP WHEN WE SAW WHAT WAS INSIDE THE CASTLE WALLS.
I EXPECTED MAYBE A MAD SCIENTIST'S LAB, OR SOME KIND OF ARMAMENT FACTORY, OR MAYBE EVEN DRACULA'S LAIR.
WHAT I DIDN'T EXPECT WAS --
AN OUT-SOURCED OVERSEAS TELEPHONE SUPPORT CALL CENTER?
SERIOUSLY?

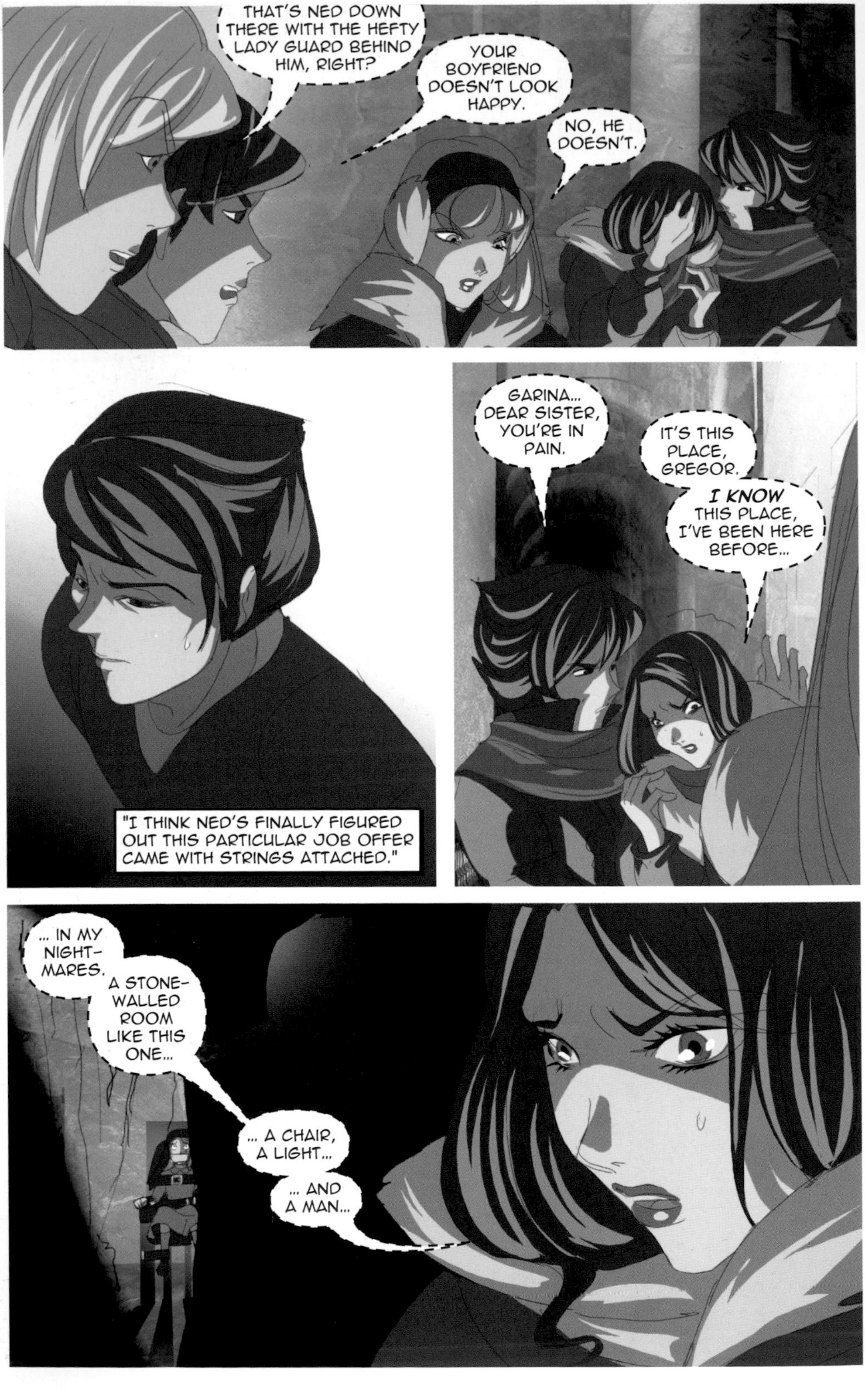
THAT'S NED DOWN THERE WITH THE HEFTY LADY GUARD BEHIND HIM, RIGHT?
YOUR BOYFRIEND DOESN'T LOOK HAPPY.
NO, HE DOESN'T.
"I THINK NED'S FINALLY FIGURED OUT THIS PARTICULAR JOB OFFER CAME WITH STRINGS ATTACHED."
GARINA... DEAR SISTER, YOU'RE IN PAIN.
IT'S THIS PLACE, GREGOR.
I KNOW THIS PLACE, I'VE BEEN HERE BEFORE...
... IN MY NIGHT-MARES.
A STONE-WALLED ROOM LIKE THIS ONE...
... A CHAIR, A LIGHT...
... AND A MAN...

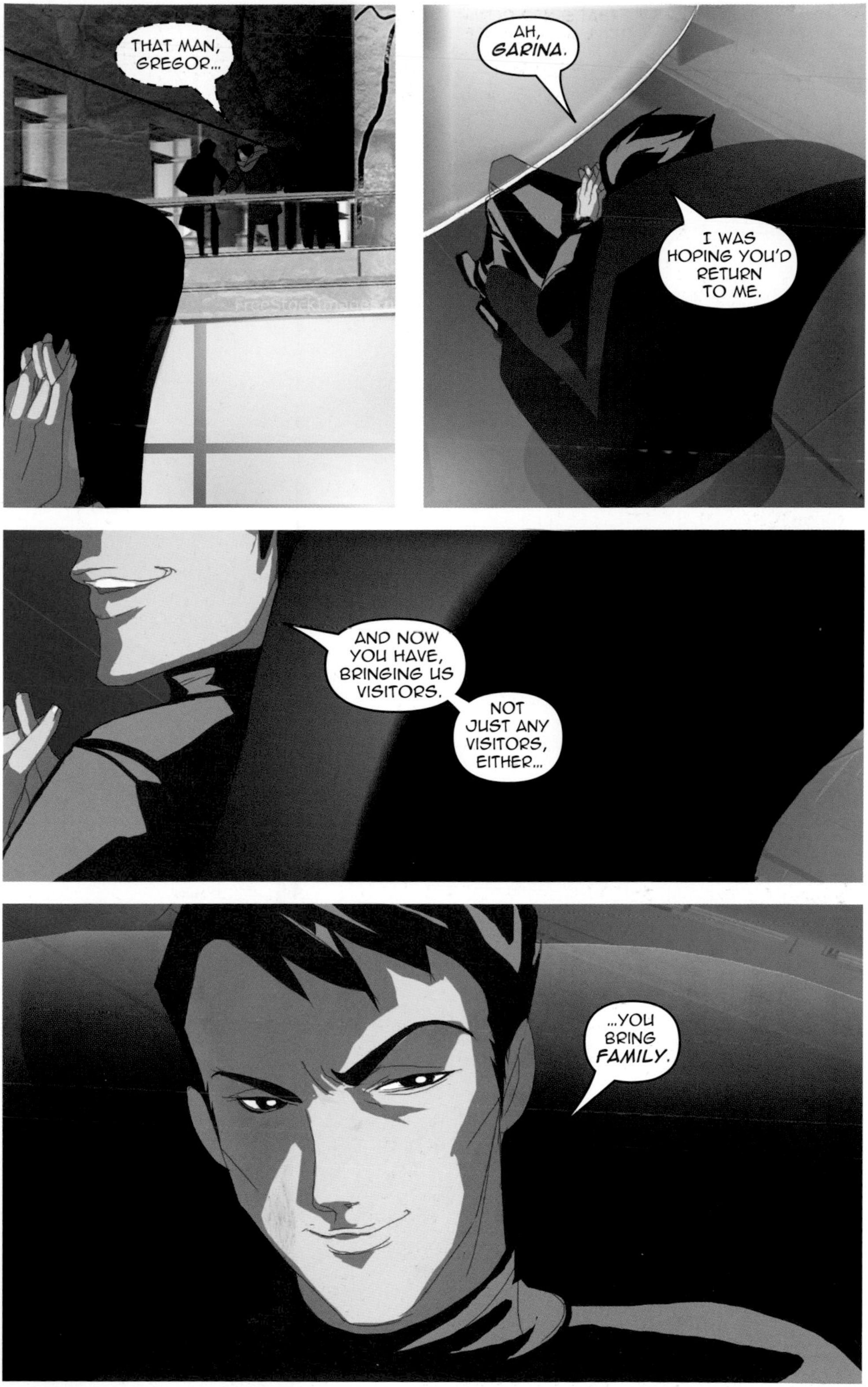
THAT MAN, GREGOR...
AH, GARINA.
I WAS HOPING YOU'D RETURN TO ME.
AND NOW YOU HAVE, BRINGING US VISITORS.
NOT JUST ANY VISITORS, EITHER...
...YOU BRING FAMILY.

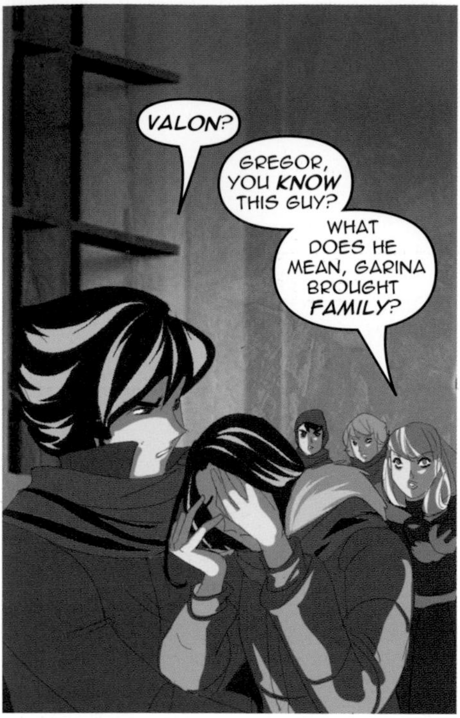
VALON?
GREGOR, YOU KNOW THIS GUY?
WHAT DOES HE MEAN, GARINA BROUGHT FAMILY?

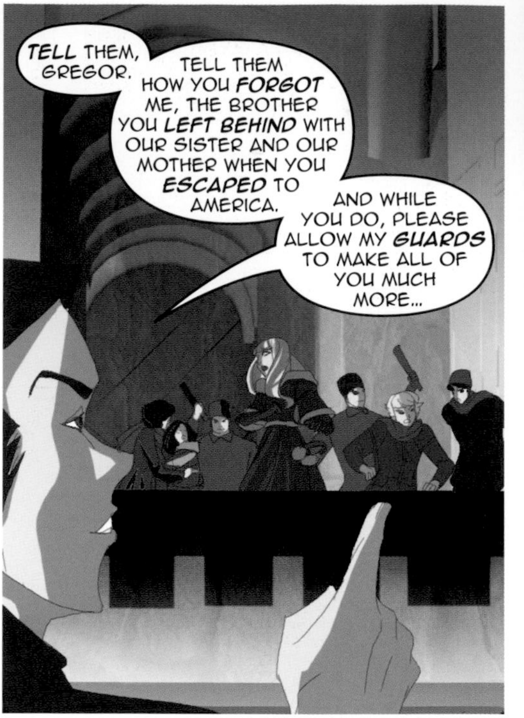
TELL THEM, GREGOR.
TELL THEM HOW YOU FORGOT ME, THE BROTHER YOU LEFT BEHIND WITH OUR SISTER AND OUR MOTHER WHEN YOU ESCAPED TO AMERICA.
AND WHILE YOU DO, PLEASE ALLOW MY GUARDS TO MAKE ALL OF YOU MUCH MORE...

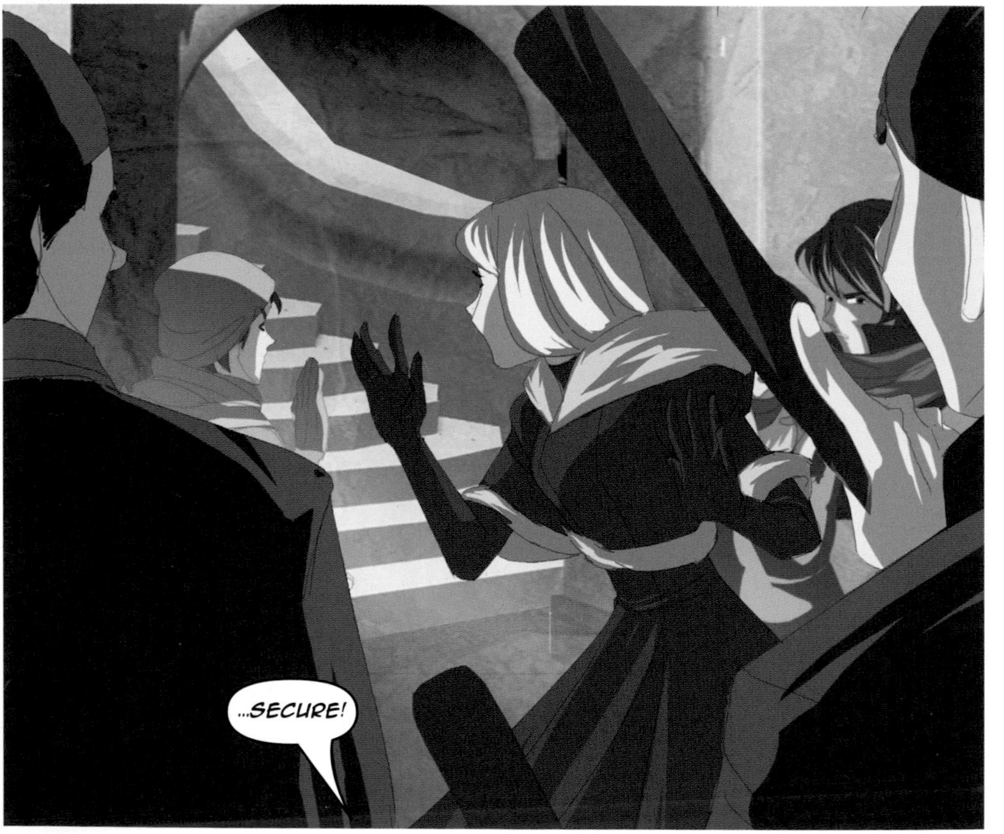
...SECURE!

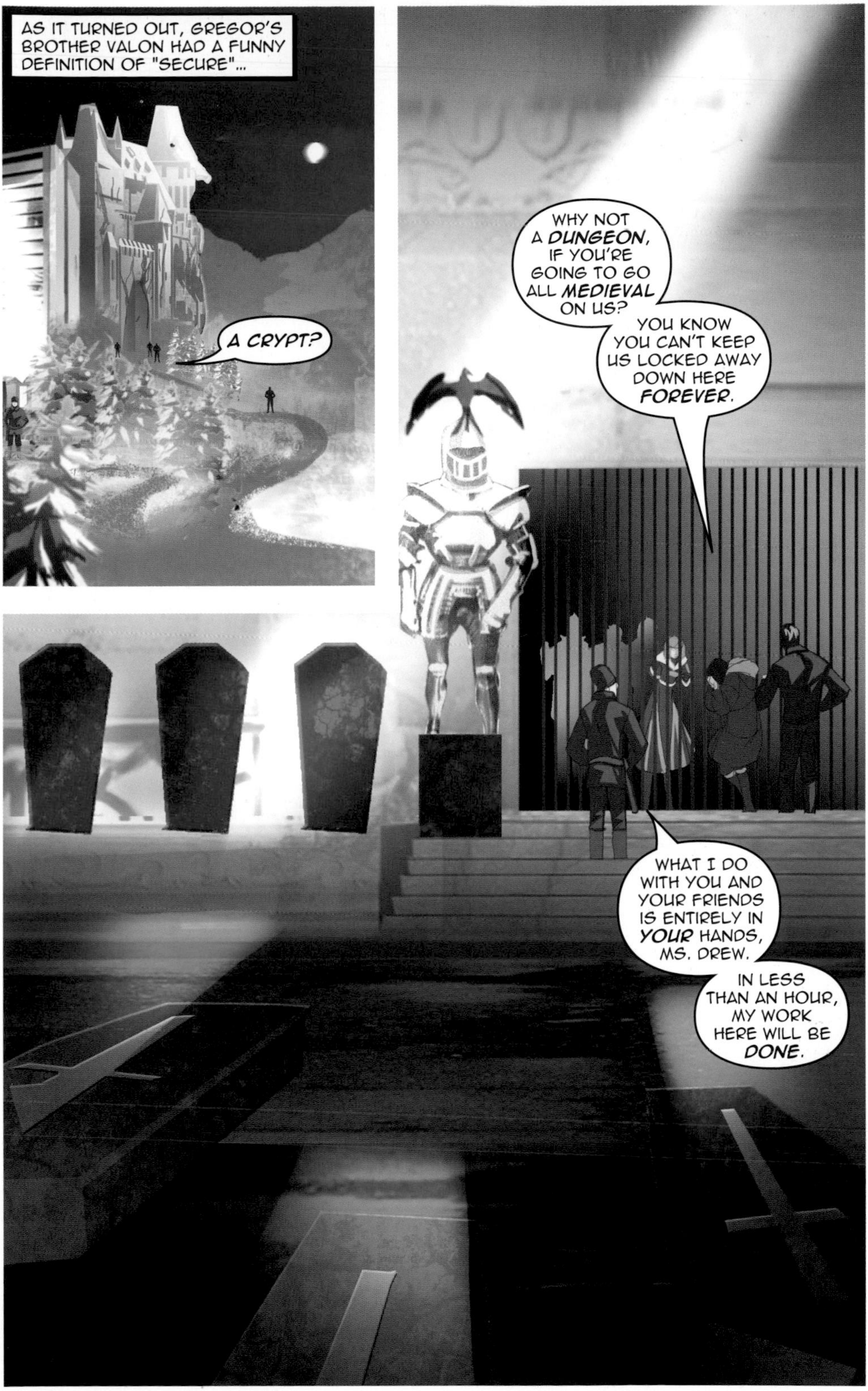

AS IT TURNED OUT, GREGOR'S BROTHER VALON HAD A FUNNY DEFINITION OF "SECURE"...
A CRYPT?
WHY NOT A DUNGEON, IF YOU'RE GOING TO GO ALL MEDIEVAL ON US?
YOU KNOW YOU CAN'T KEEP US LOCKED AWAY DOWN HERE FOREVER.
WHAT I DO WITH YOU AND YOUR FRIENDS IS ENTIRELY IN YOUR HANDS, MS. DREW.
IN LESS THAN AN HOUR, MY WORK HERE WILL BE DONE.

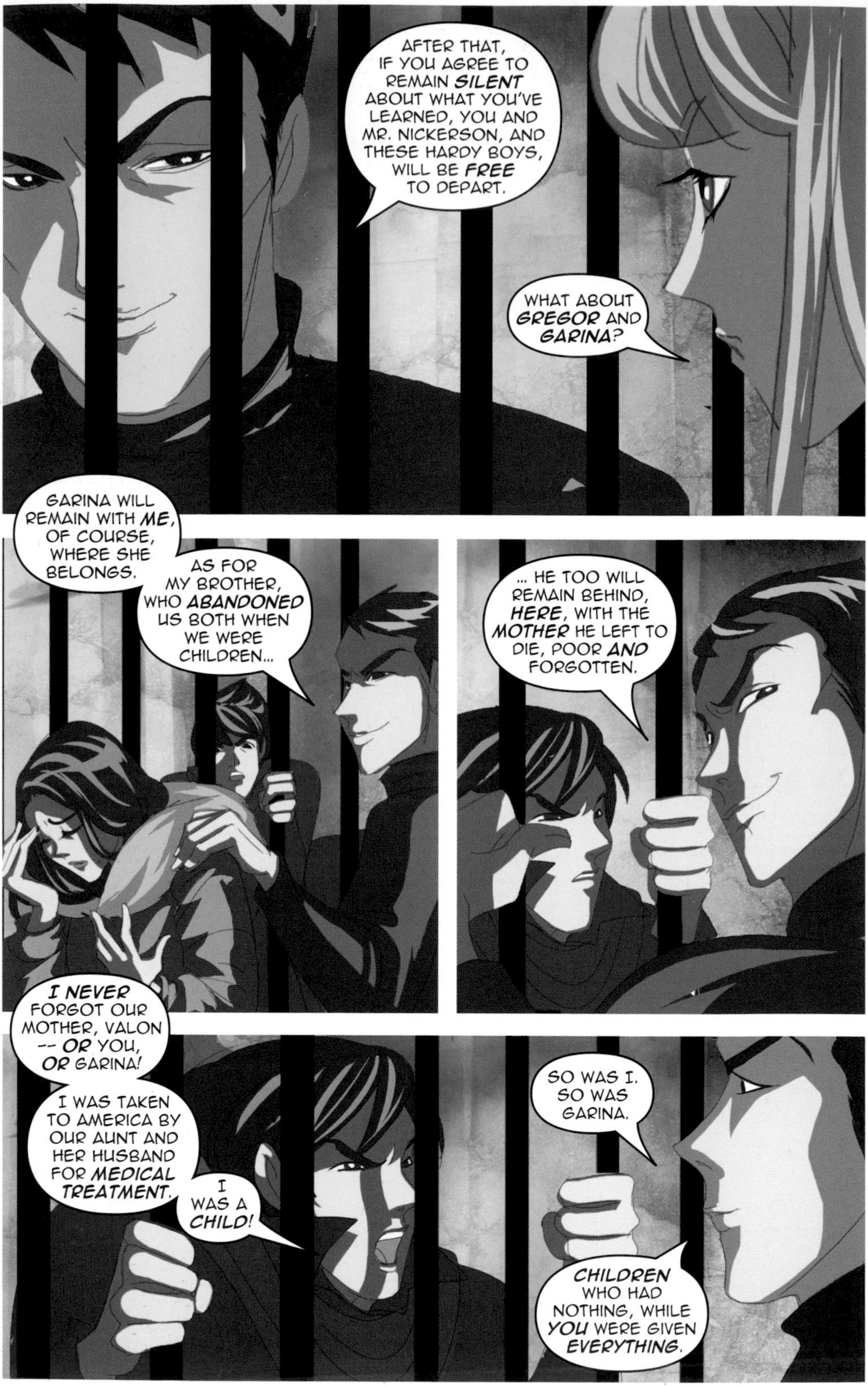
AFTER THAT, IF YOU AGREE TO REMAIN SILENT ABOUT WHAT YOU'VE LEARNED, YOU AND MR. NICKERSON, AND THESE HARDY BOYS, WILL BE FREE TO DEPART.
WHAT ABOUT GREGOR AND GARINA?
GARINA WILL REMAIN WITH ME, OF COURSE, WHERE SHE BELONGS.
AS FOR MY BROTHER, WHO ABANDONED US BOTH WHEN WE WERE CHILDREN...
... HE TOO WILL REMAIN BEHIND, HERE, WITH THE MOTHER HE LEFT TO DIE, POOR AND FORGOTTEN.
I NEVER FORGOT OUR MOTHER, VALON -- OR YOU, OR GARINA!
I WAS TAKEN TO AMERICA BY OUR AUNT AND HER HUSBAND FOR MEDICAL TREATMENT.
I WAS A CHILD!
SO WAS I. SO WAS GARINA.
CHILDREN WHO HAD NOTHING, WHILE YOU WERE GIVEN EVERYTHING.

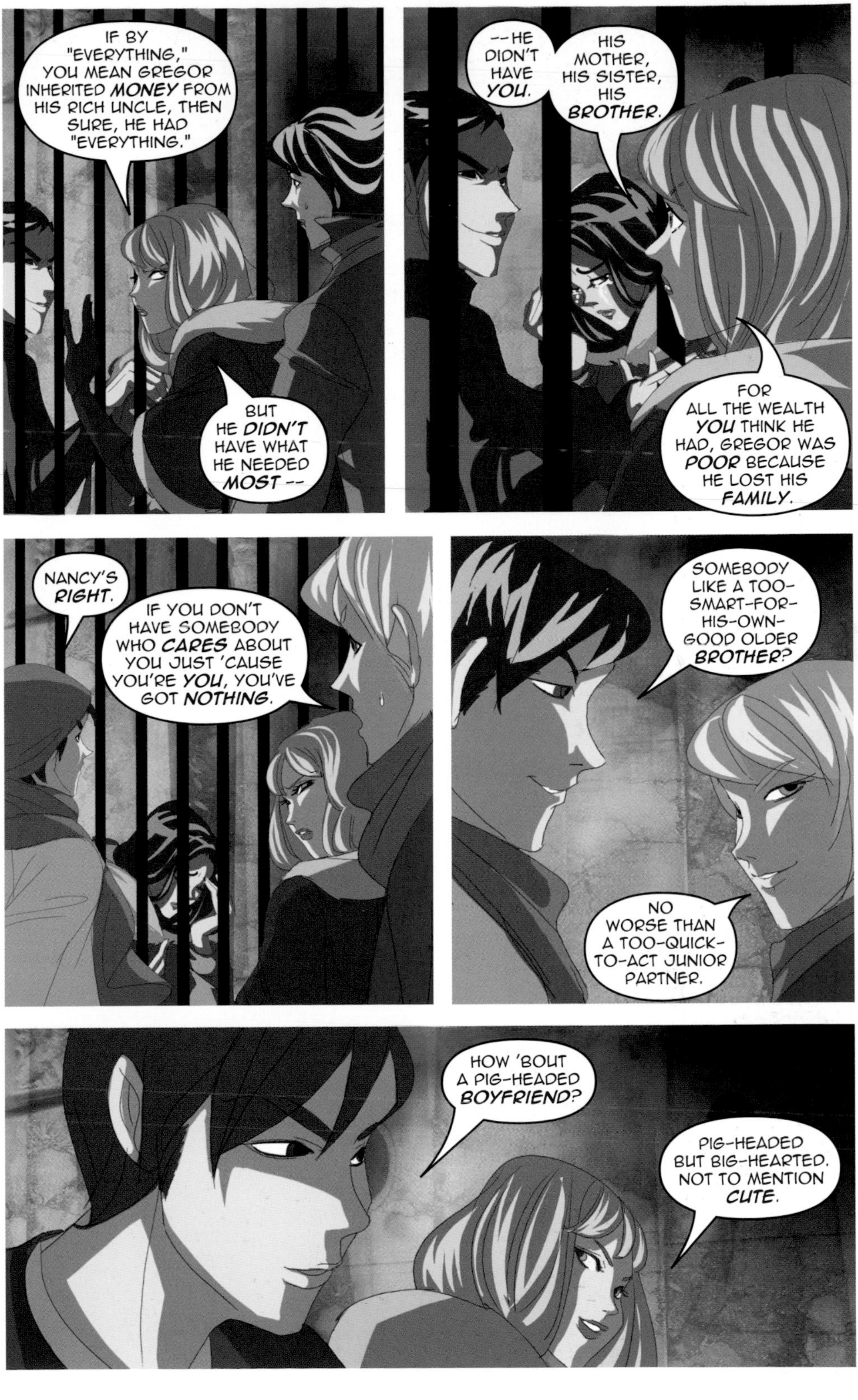
IF BY "EVERYTHING," YOU MEAN GREGOR INHERITED MONEY FROM HIS RICH UNCLE, THEN SURE, HE HAD "EVERYTHING."
BUT HE DIDN'T HAVE WHAT HE NEEDED MOST --
--HE DIDN'T HAVE YOU.
HIS MOTHER, HIS SISTER, HIS BROTHER.
FOR ALL THE WEALTH YOU THINK HE HAD, GREGOR WAS POOR BECAUSE HE LOST HIS FAMILY.
NANCY'S RIGHT.
IF YOU DON'T HAVE SOMEBODY WHO CARES ABOUT YOU JUST 'CAUSE YOU'RE YOU, YOU'VE GOT NOTHING.
SOMEBODY LIKE A TOO-SMART-FOR-HIS-OWN-GOOD OLDER BROTHER?
NO WORSE THAN A TOO-QUICK-TO-ACT JUNIOR PARTNER.
HOW 'BOUT A PIG-HEADED BOYFRIEND?
PIG-HEADED BUT BIG-HEARTED. NOT TO MENTION CUTE.

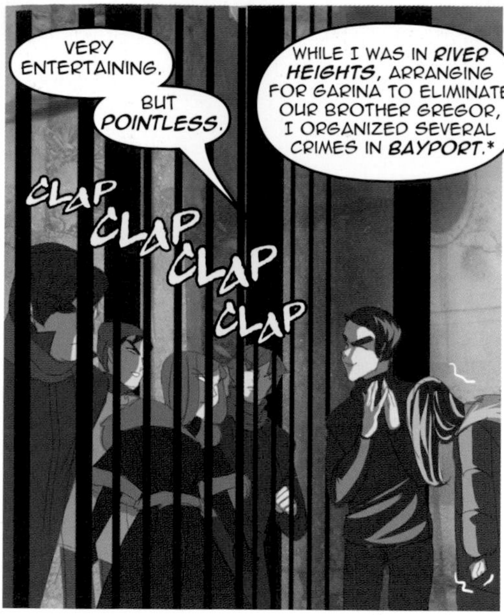
VERY ENTERTAINING.
BUT POINTLESS.
CLAP CLAP CLAP CLAP
WHILE I WAS IN RIVER HEIGHTS, ARRANGING FOR GARINA TO ELIMINATE OUR BROTHER GREGOR, I ORGANIZED SEVERAL CRIMES IN BAYPORT.*

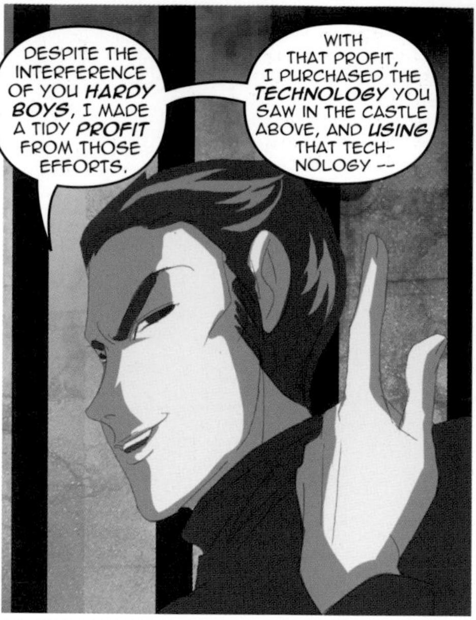
DESPITE THE INTERFERENCE OF YOU HARDY BOYS, I MADE A TIDY PROFIT FROM THOSE EFFORTS.
WITH THAT PROFIT, I PURCHASED THE TECHNOLOGY YOU SAW IN THE CASTLE ABOVE, AND USING THAT TECH-NOLOGY --

*AS TOLD IN ***THE HARDY BOYS*** THE NEW CASE FILES #1 & #2.

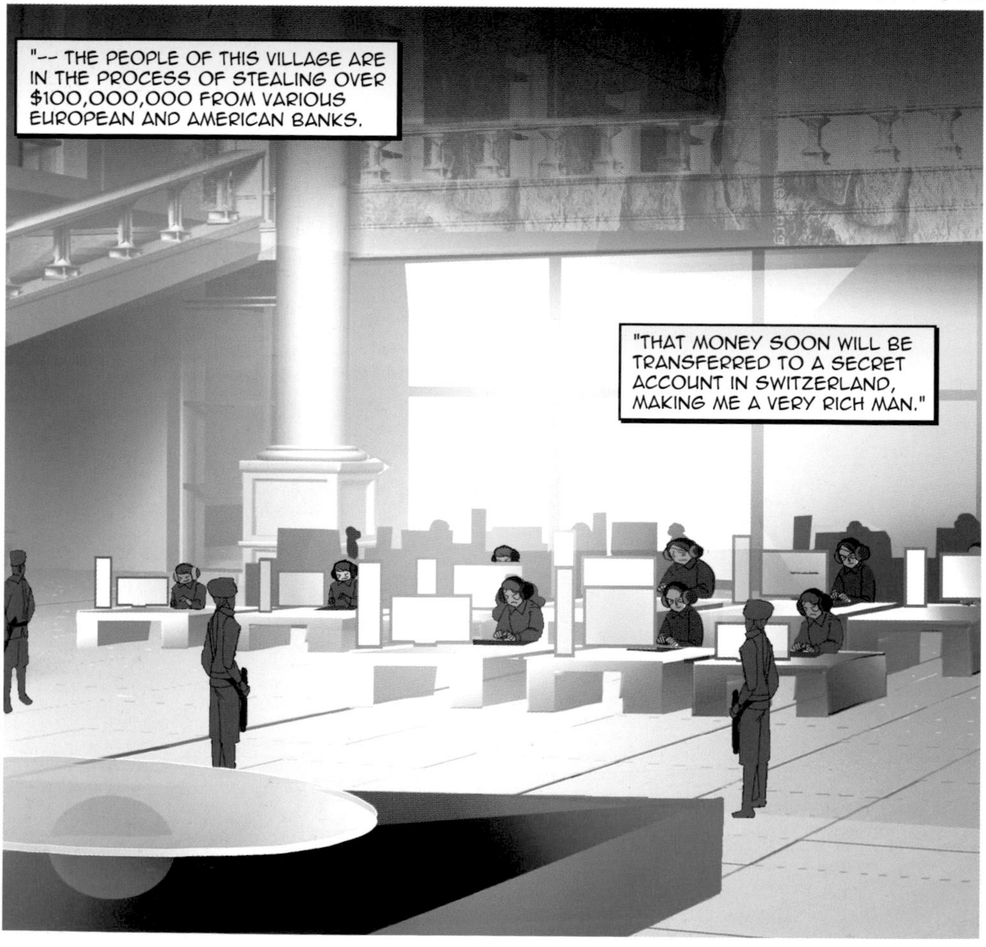
"-- THE PEOPLE OF THIS VILLAGE ARE IN THE PROCESS OF STEALING OVER $100,000,000 FROM VARIOUS EUROPEAN AND AMERICAN BANKS.
"THAT MONEY SOON WILL BE TRANSFERRED TO A SECRET ACCOUNT IN SWITZERLAND, MAKING ME A VERY RICH MAN."

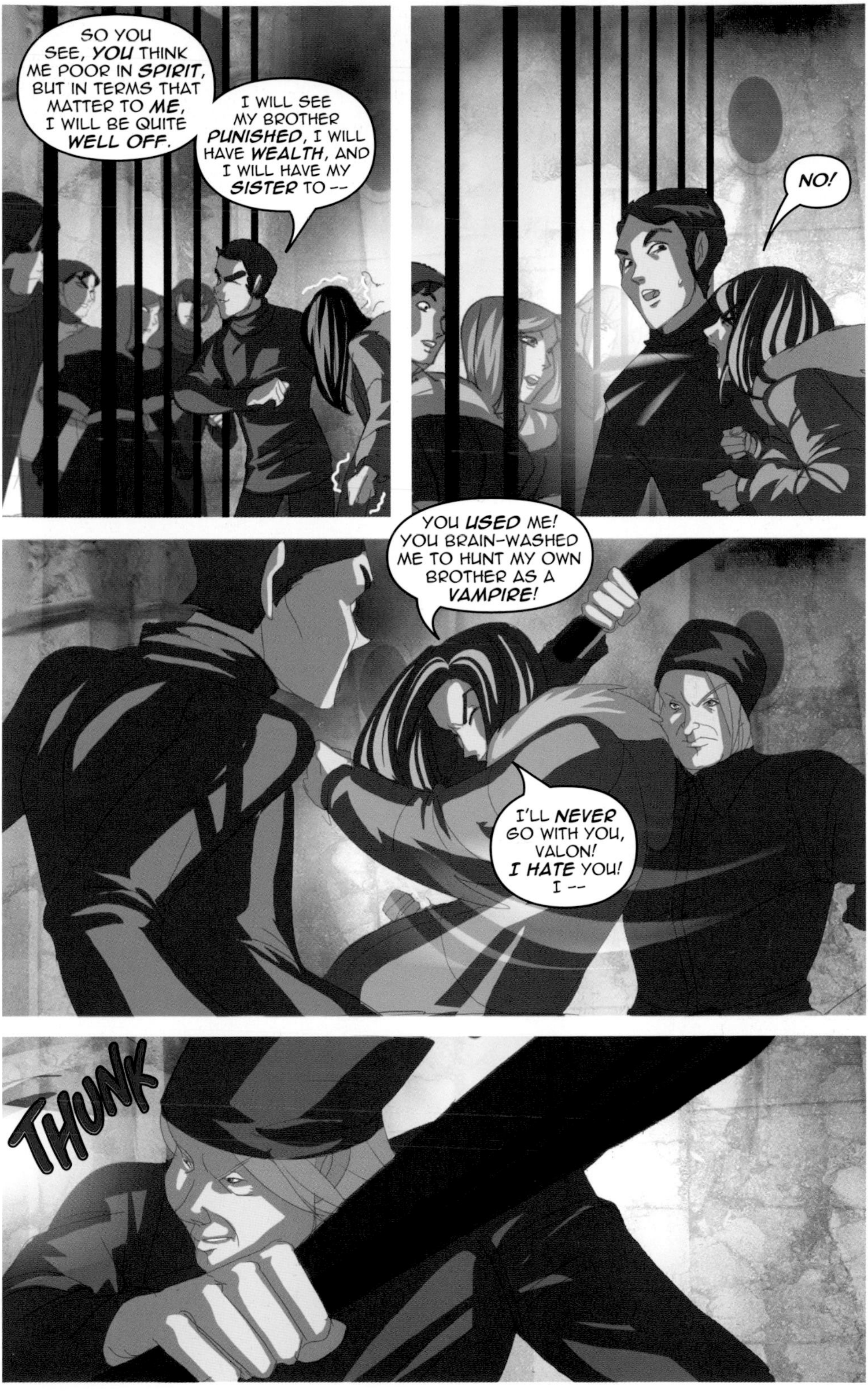
SO YOU SEE, YOU THINK ME POOR IN SPIRIT, BUT IN TERMS THAT MATTER TO ME, I WILL BE QUITE WELL OFF.
I WILL SEE MY BROTHER PUNISHED, I WILL HAVE WEALTH, AND I WILL HAVE MY SISTER TO --
NO!
YOU USED ME! YOU BRAIN-WASHED ME TO HUNT MY OWN BROTHER AS A VAMPIRE!
I'LL NEVER GO WITH YOU, VALON! I HATE YOU! I --
THUNK

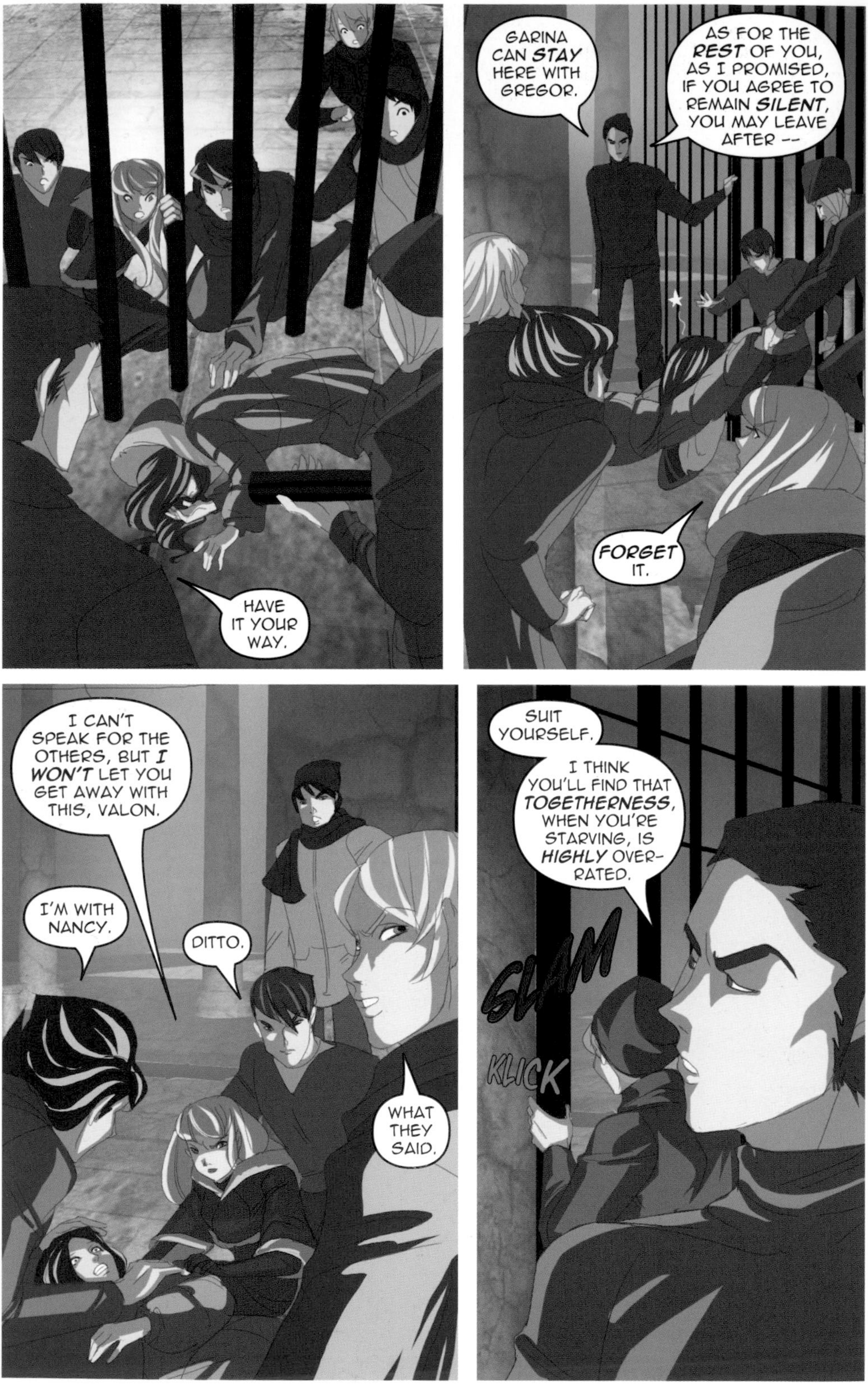
HAVE IT YOUR WAY.
GARINA CAN STAY HERE WITH GREGOR.
AS FOR THE REST OF YOU, AS I PROMISED, IF YOU AGREE TO REMAIN SILENT, YOU MAY LEAVE AFTER --
FORGET IT.
I CAN'T SPEAK FOR THE OTHERS, BUT I WON'T LET YOU GET AWAY WITH THIS, VALON.
I'M WITH NANCY.
DITTO.
WHAT THEY SAID.
SUIT YOURSELF.
I THINK YOU'LL FIND THAT TOGETHERNESS, WHEN YOU'RE STARVING, IS HIGHLY OVER-RATED.
SLAM
KLICK

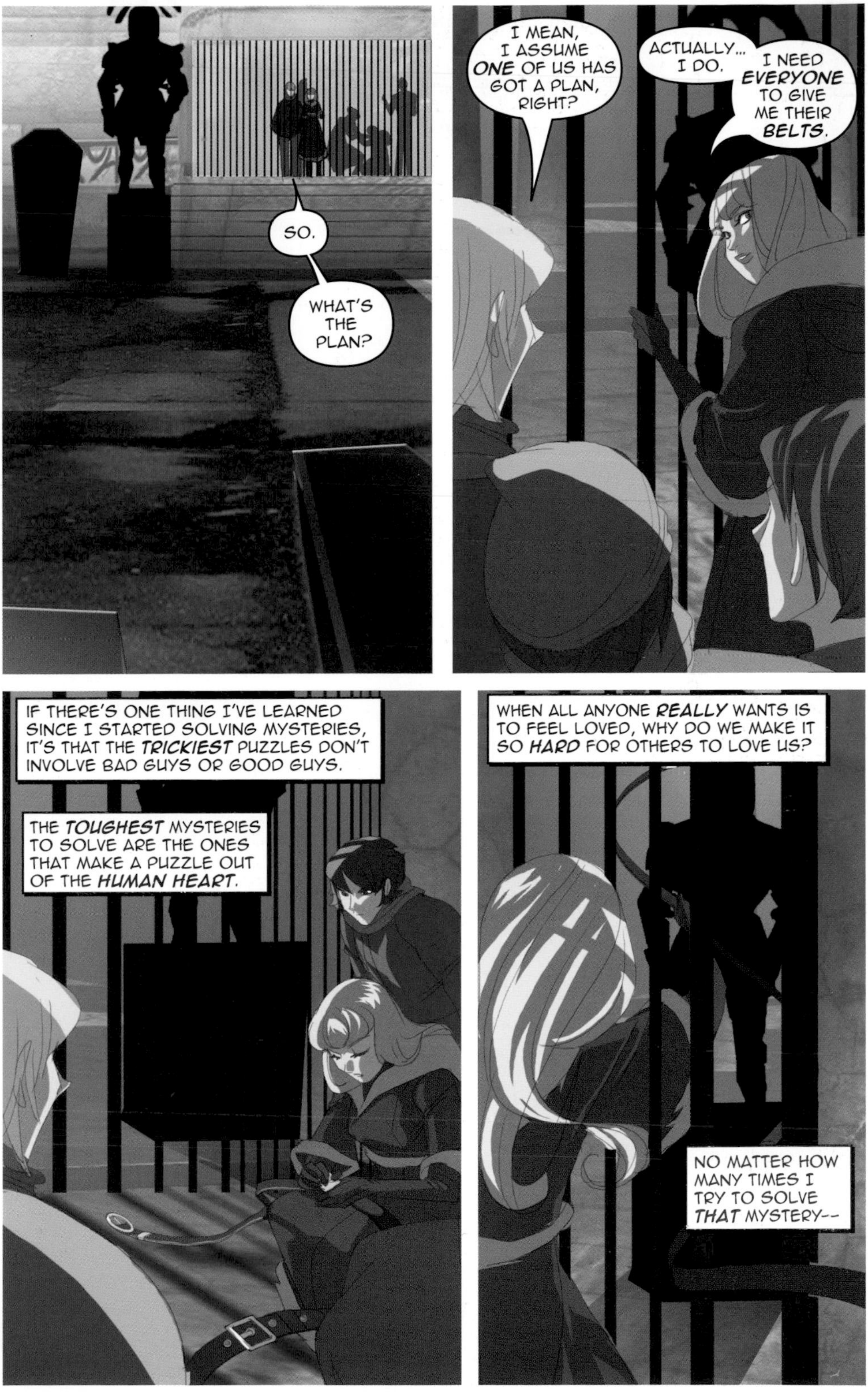
SO.
WHAT'S THE PLAN?
I MEAN, I ASSUME ONE OF US HAS GOT A PLAN, RIGHT?
ACTUALLY... I DO.
I NEED EVERYONE TO GIVE ME THEIR BELTS.
IF THERE'S ONE THING I'VE LEARNED SINCE I STARTED SOLVING MYSTERIES, IT'S THAT THE TRICKIEST PUZZLES DON'T INVOLVE BAD GUYS OR GOOD GUYS.
THE TOUGHEST MYSTERIES TO SOLVE ARE THE ONES THAT MAKE A PUZZLE OUT OF THE HUMAN HEART.
WHEN ALL ANYONE REALLY WANTS IS TO FEEL LOVED, WHY DO WE MAKE IT SO HARD FOR OTHERS TO LOVE US?
NO MATTER HOW MANY TIMES I TRY TO SOLVE THAT MYSTERY--

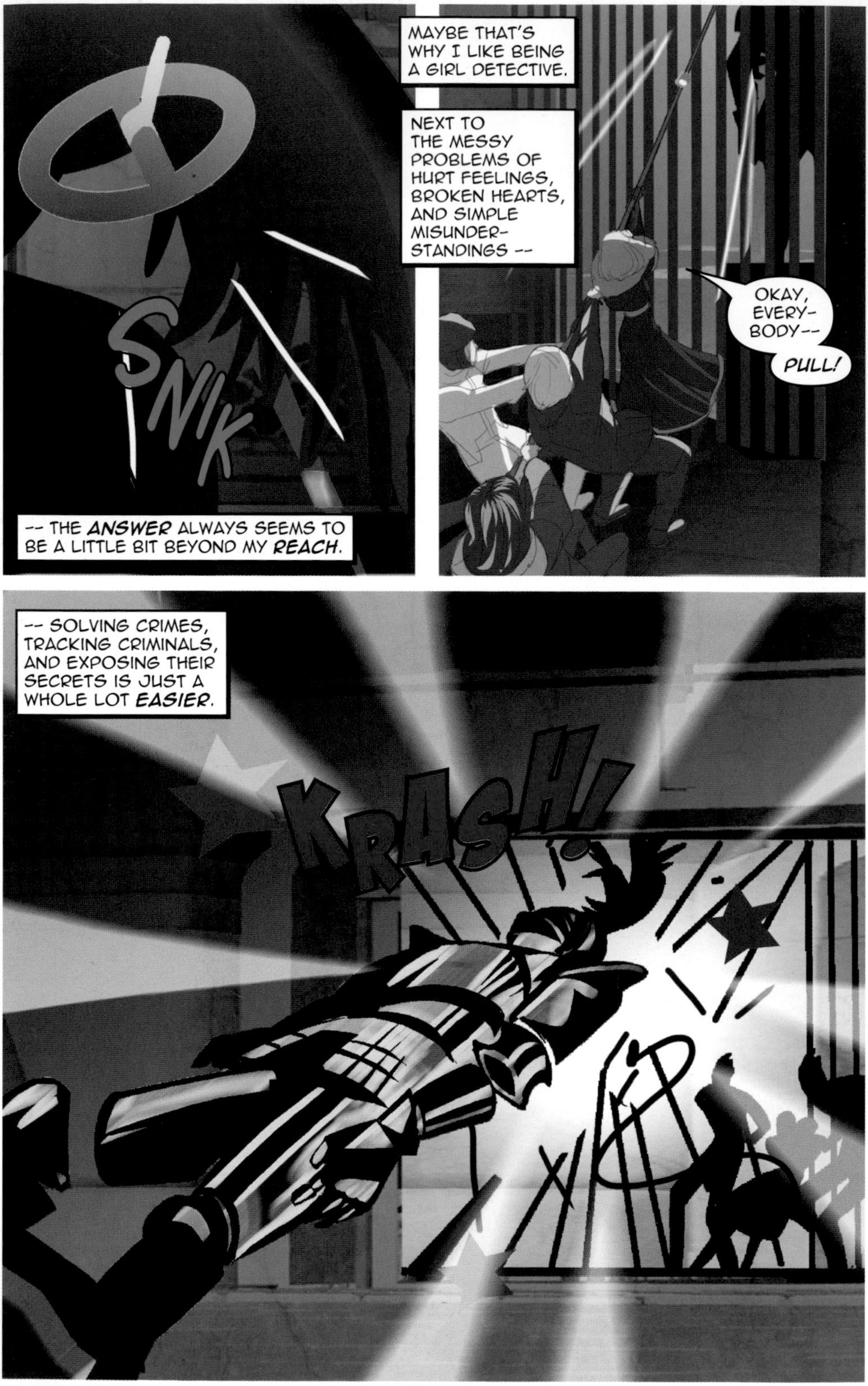
SNIK
-- THE ANSWER ALWAYS SEEMS TO BE A LITTLE BIT BEYOND MY REACH.
MAYBE THAT'S WHY I LIKE BEING A GIRL DETECTIVE.
NEXT TO THE MESSY PROBLEMS OF HURT FEELINGS, BROKEN HEARTS, AND SIMPLE MISUNDER-STANDINGS --
OKAY, EVERY-BODY--
PULL!
-- SOLVING CRIMES, TRACKING CRIMINALS, AND EXPOSING THEIR SECRETS IS JUST A WHOLE LOT EASIER.
KRASH!

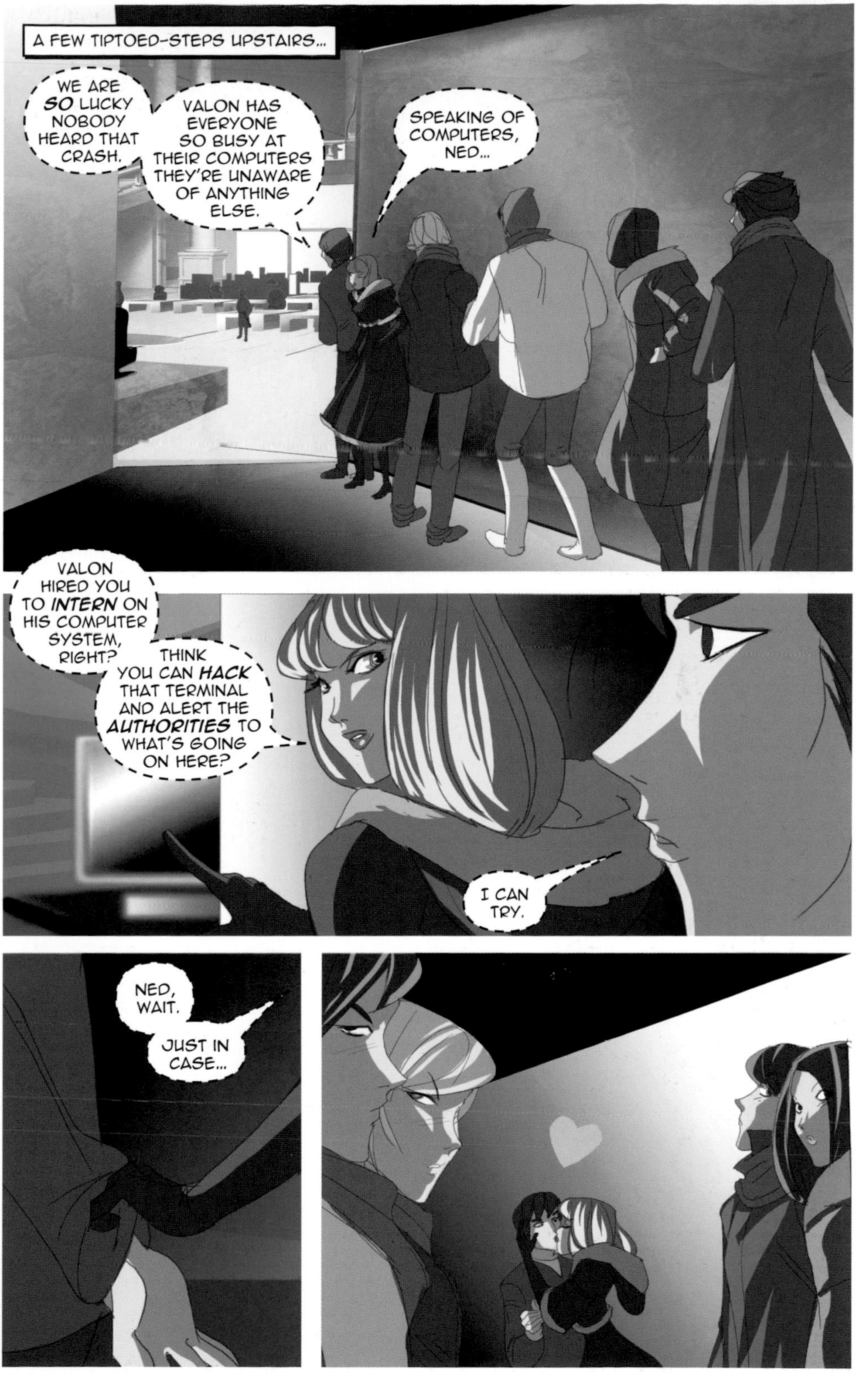
A FEW TIPTOED-STEPS UPSTAIRS...
WE ARE SO LUCKY NOBODY HEARD THAT CRASH.
VALON HAS EVERYONE SO BUSY AT THEIR COMPUTERS THEY'RE UNAWARE OF ANYTHING ELSE.
SPEAKING OF COMPUTERS, NED...
VALON HIRED YOU TO INTERN ON HIS COMPUTER SYSTEM, RIGHT?
THINK YOU CAN HACK THAT TERMINAL AND ALERT THE AUTHORITIES TO WHAT'S GOING ON HERE?
I CAN TRY.
NED, WAIT.
JUST IN CASE...

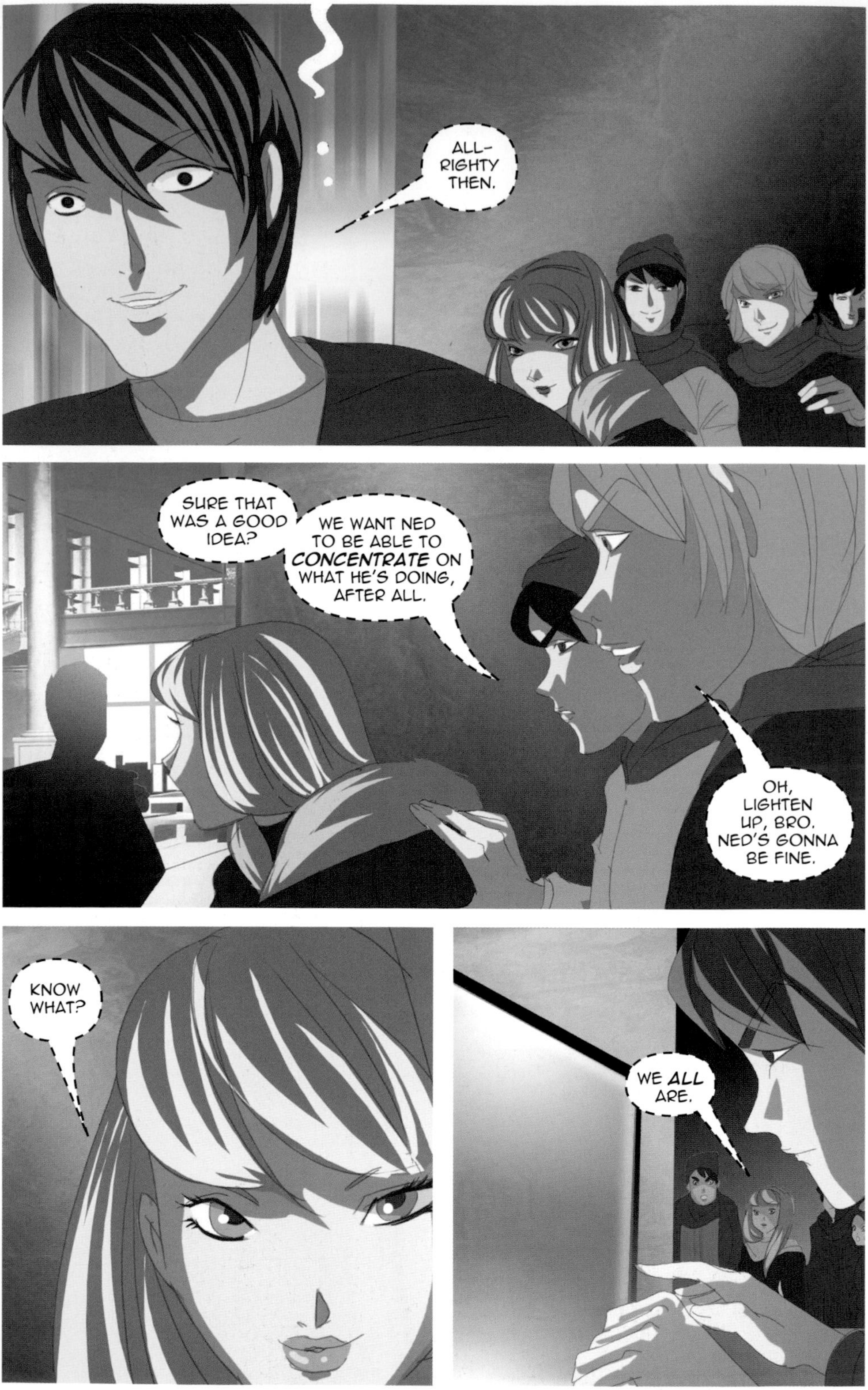
ALL-RIGHTY THEN.
SURE THAT WAS A GOOD IDEA?
WE WANT NED TO BE ABLE TO CONCENTRATE ON WHAT HE'S DOING, AFTER ALL.
OH, LIGHTEN UP, BRO. NED'S GONNA BE FINE.
KNOW WHAT?
WE ALL ARE.

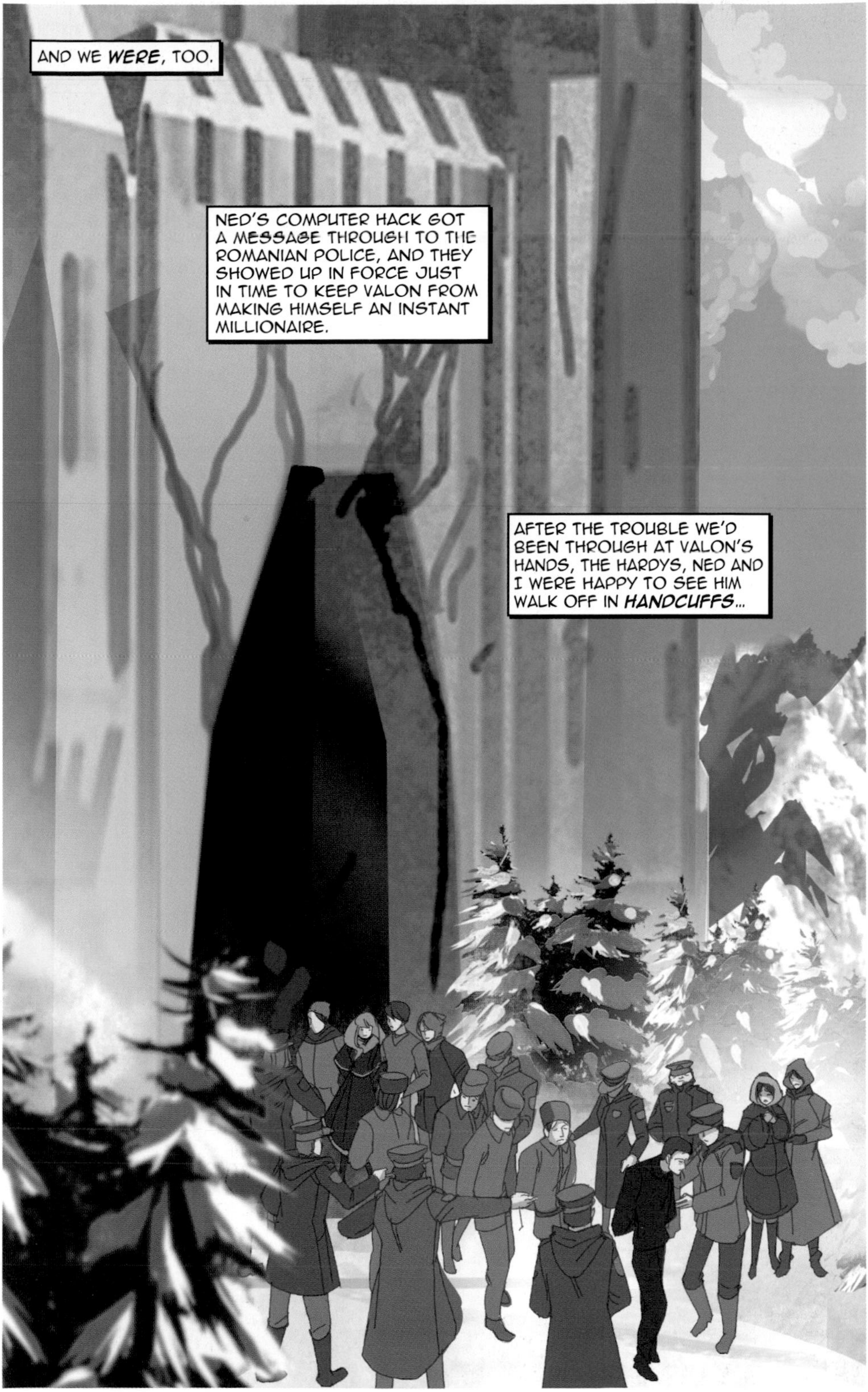
AND WE *WERE*, TOO.
NED'S COMPUTER HACK GOT A MESSAGE THROUGH TO THE ROMANIAN POLICE, AND THEY SHOWED UP IN FORCE JUST IN TIME TO KEEP VALON FROM MAKING HIMSELF AN INSTANT MILLIONAIRE.
AFTER THE TROUBLE WE'D BEEN THROUGH AT VALON'S HANDS, THE HARDYS, NED AND I WERE HAPPY TO SEE HIM WALK OFF IN *HANDCUFFS*...

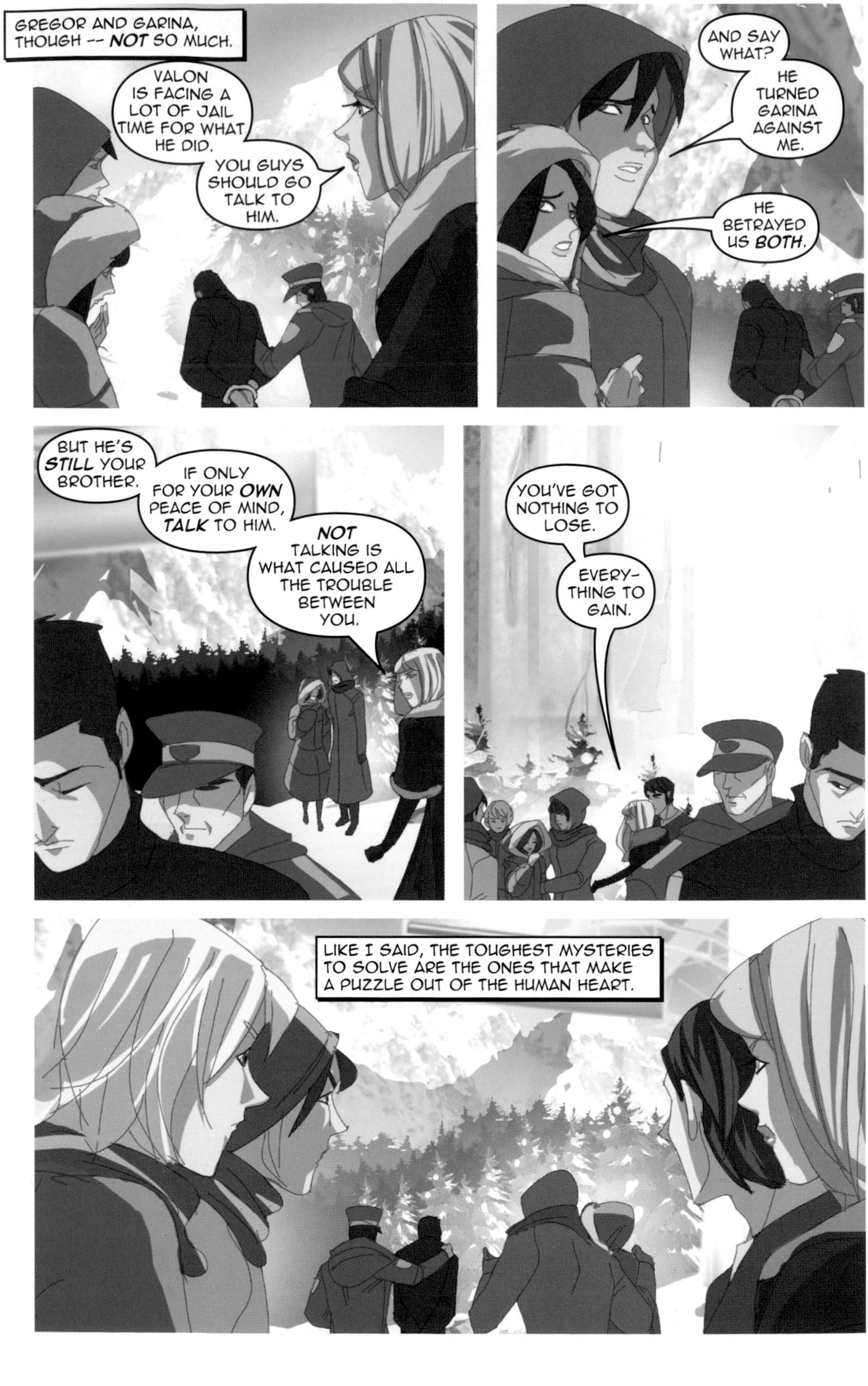
GREGOR AND GARINA, THOUGH -- **NOT** SO MUCH.
VALON IS FACING A LOT OF JAIL TIME FOR WHAT HE DID.
YOU GUYS SHOULD GO TALK TO HIM.
AND SAY WHAT?
HE TURNED GARINA AGAINST ME.
HE BETRAYED US **BOTH**.
BUT HE'S **STILL** YOUR BROTHER.
IF ONLY FOR YOUR **OWN** PEACE OF MIND, **TALK** TO HIM.
NOT TALKING IS WHAT CAUSED ALL THE TROUBLE BETWEEN YOU.
YOU'VE GOT NOTHING TO LOSE.
EVERY-THING TO GAIN.
LIKE I SAID, THE TOUGHEST MYSTERIES TO SOLVE ARE THE ONES THAT MAKE A PUZZLE OUT OF THE HUMAN HEART.

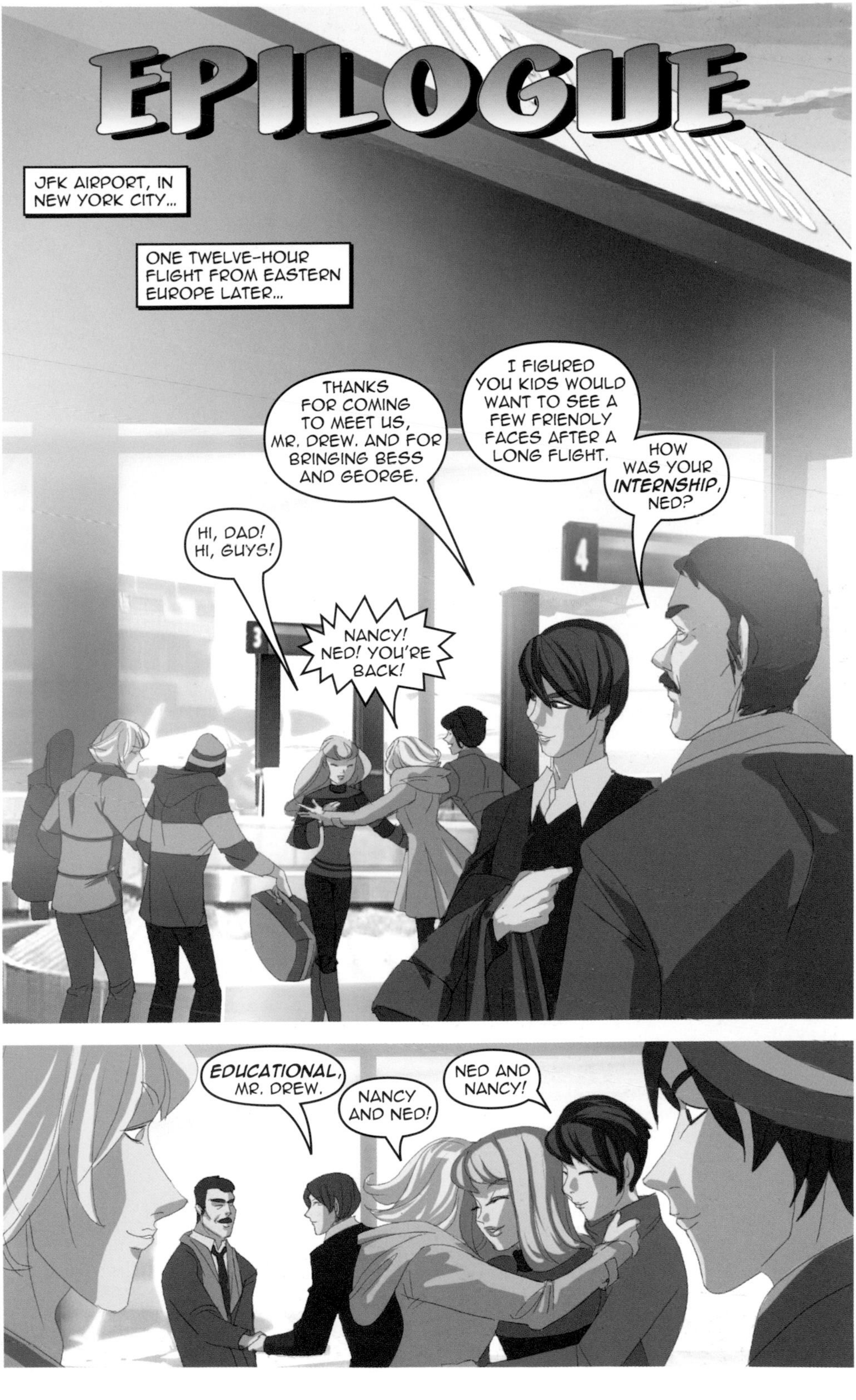
EPILOGUE
JFK AIRPORT, IN NEW YORK CITY...
ONE TWELVE-HOUR FLIGHT FROM EASTERN EUROPE LATER...
HI, DAD! HI, GUYS!
NANCY! NED! YOU'RE BACK!
THANKS FOR COMING TO MEET US, MR. DREW. AND FOR BRINGING BESS AND GEORGE.
I FIGURED YOU KIDS WOULD WANT TO SEE A FEW FRIENDLY FACES AFTER A LONG FLIGHT.
HOW WAS YOUR *INTERNSHIP*, NED?
4
3
EDUCATIONAL, MR. DREW.
NANCY AND NED!
NED AND NANCY!

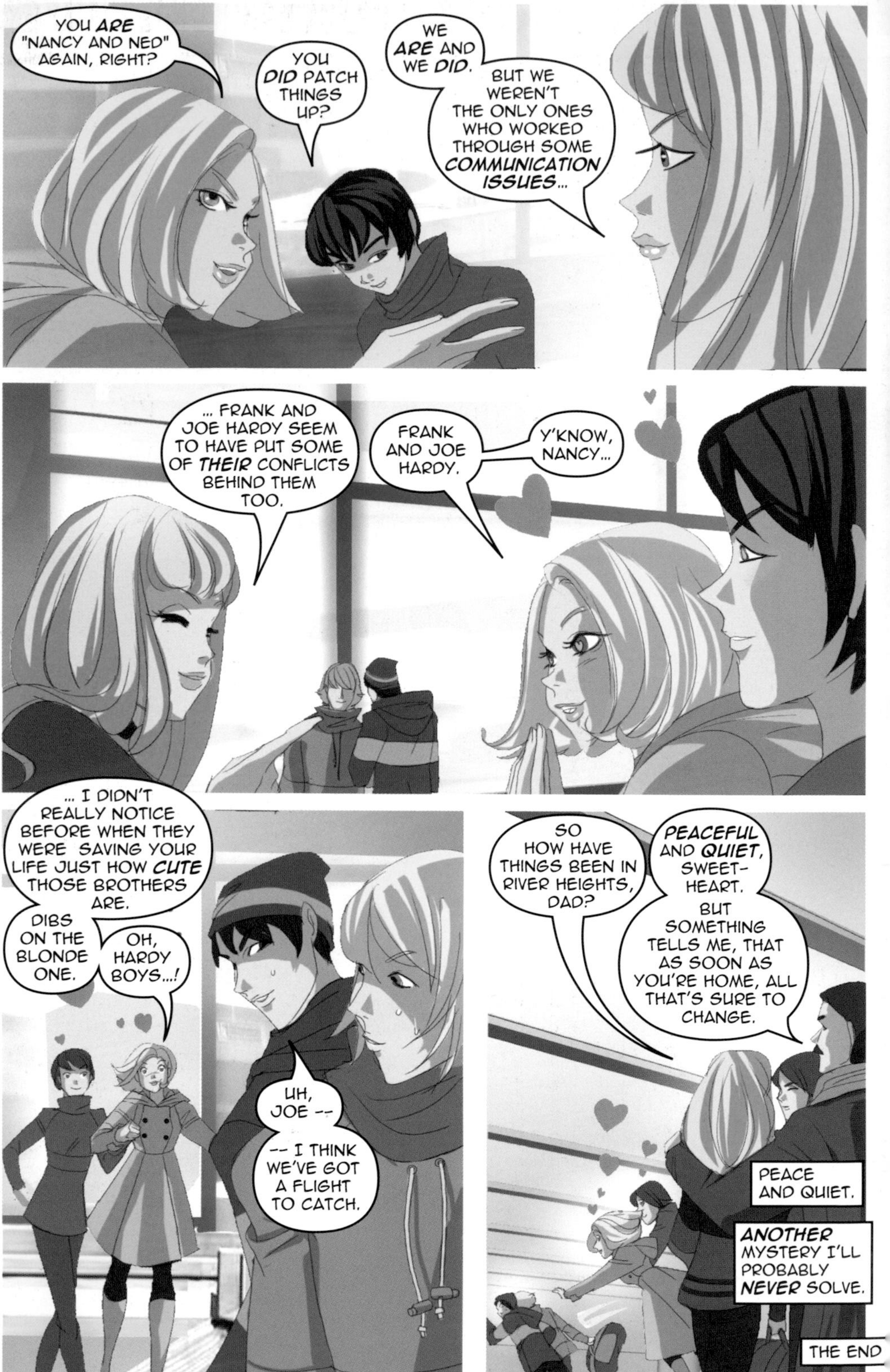
YOU ARE "NANCY AND NED" AGAIN, RIGHT?
YOU DID PATCH THINGS UP?
WE ARE AND WE DID.
BUT WE WEREN'T THE ONLY ONES WHO WORKED THROUGH SOME COMMUNICATION ISSUES...
... FRANK AND JOE HARDY SEEM TO HAVE PUT SOME OF THEIR CONFLICTS BEHIND THEM TOO.
FRANK AND JOE HARDY.
Y'KNOW, NANCY...
... I DIDN'T REALLY NOTICE BEFORE WHEN THEY WERE SAVING YOUR LIFE JUST HOW CUTE THOSE BROTHERS ARE.
DIBS ON THE BLONDE ONE.
OH, HARDY BOYS...!
UH, JOE --
-- I THINK WE'VE GOT A FLIGHT TO CATCH.
SO HOW HAVE THINGS BEEN IN RIVER HEIGHTS, DAD?
PEACEFUL AND QUIET, SWEET-HEART.
BUT SOMETHING TELLS ME, THAT AS SOON AS YOU'RE HOME, ALL THAT'S SURE TO CHANGE.
PEACE AND QUIET.
ANOTHER MYSTERY I'LL PROBABLY NEVER SOLVE.
THE END

NANCY DREW GRAPHIC NOVELS AVAILABLE FROM PAPERCUTZ

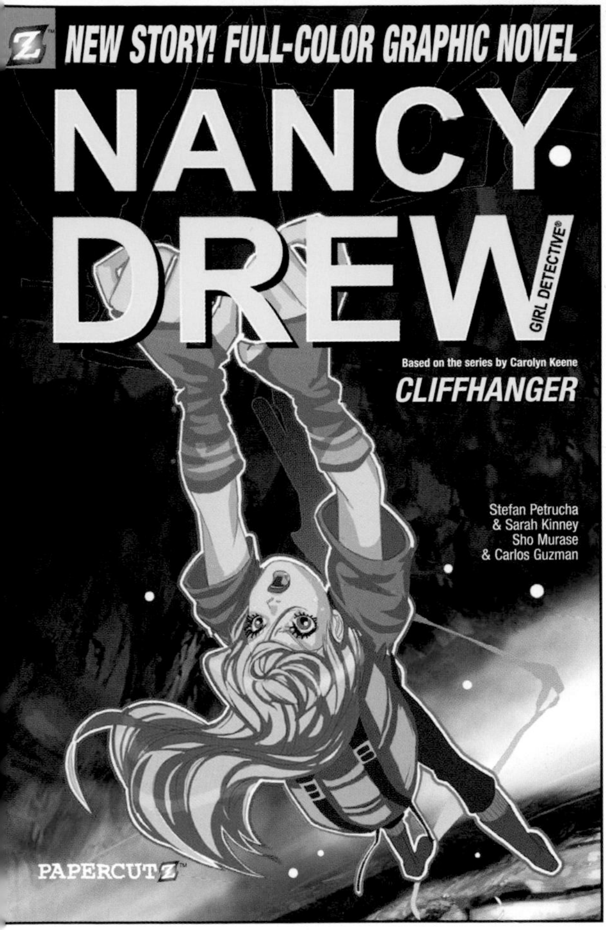
NEW STORY! FULL-COLOR GRAPHIC NOVEL
NANCY DREW
GIRL DETECTIVE
Based on the series by Carolyn Keene
CLIFFHANGER
Stefan Petrucha
& Sarah Kinney
Sho Murase
& Carlos Guzman
PAPERCUTZ

#19 "Cliffhanger"

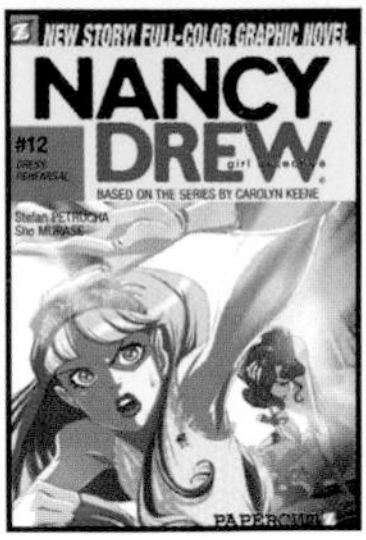
NEW STORY! FULL-COLOR GRAPHIC NOVEL
NANCY DREW
#12
BASED ON THE SERIES BY CAROLYN KEENE
PAPERCUTZ

#12 "Dress Reversal"

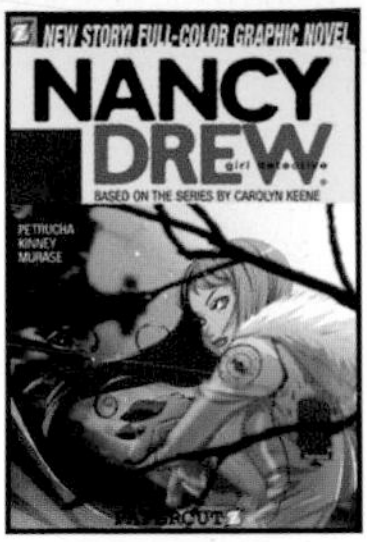
NEW STORY! FULL-COLOR GRAPHIC NOVEL
NANCY DREW
BASED ON THE SERIES BY CAROLYN KEENE
PETRUCHA
KINNEY
MURASE

#13 "Doggone Town"

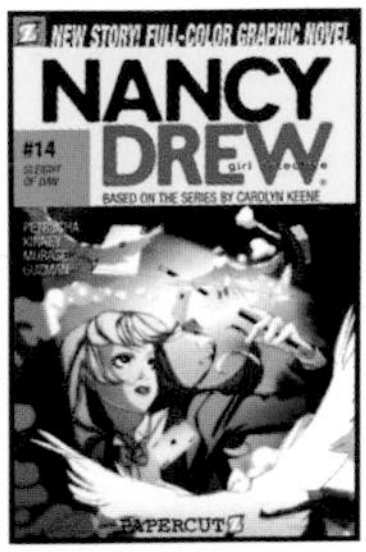
NEW STORY! FULL-COLOR GRAPHIC NOVEL
NANCY DREW
#14
BASED ON THE SERIES BY CAROLYN KEENE
PAPERCUTZ

#14 "Sleight of Dan"

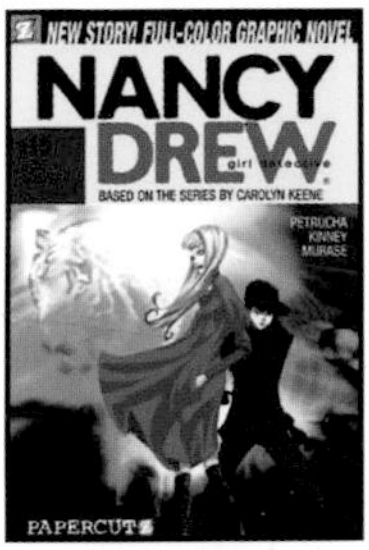
NEW STORY! FULL-COLOR GRAPHIC NOVEL
NANCY DREW
BASED ON THE SERIES BY CAROLYN KEENE
PETRUCHA
KINNEY
MURASE
PAPERCUTZ

#15 "Tiger Counter"

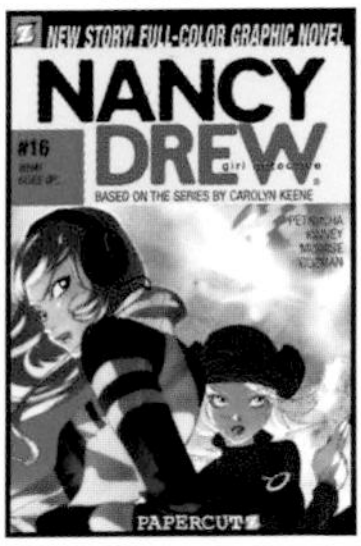
NEW STORY! FULL-COLOR GRAPHIC NOVEL
NANCY DREW
#16
BASED ON THE SERIES BY CAROLYN KEENE
PAPERCUTZ

#16 "What Goes Up..."

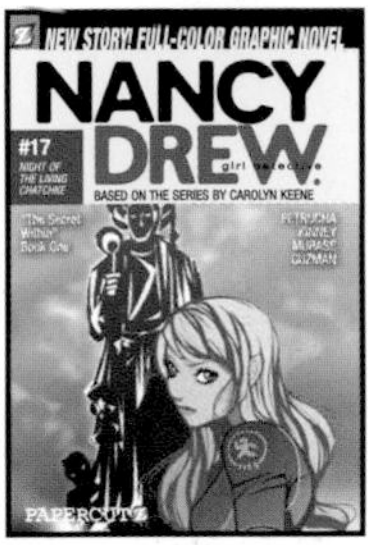
NEW STORY! FULL-COLOR GRAPHIC NOVEL
NANCY DREW
#17
BASED ON THE SERIES BY CAROLYN KEENE
PAPERCUTZ

#17 "Night of the Living Chatchke"

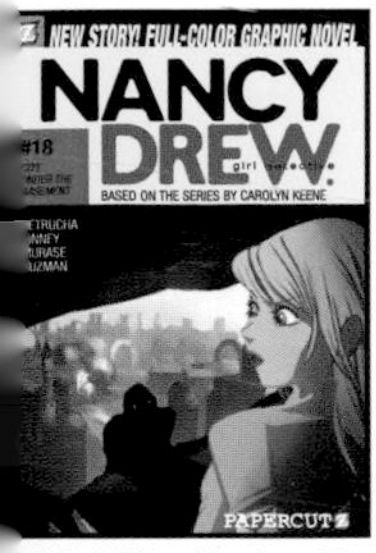
NEW STORY! FULL-COLOR GRAPHIC NOVEL
NANCY DREW
#18
BASED ON THE SERIES BY CAROLYN KEENE
PAPERCUTZ

#18 "City Under the Basement"

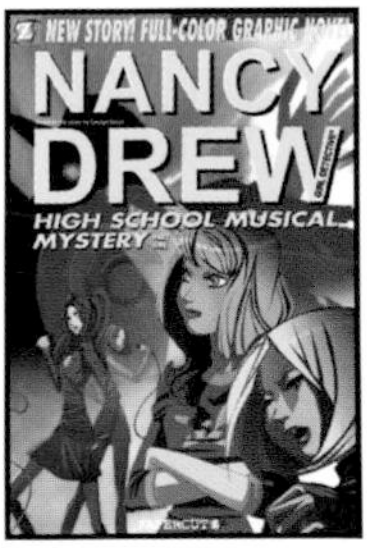
NEW STORY! FULL-COLOR GRAPHIC NOVEL
NANCY DREW
HIGH SCHOOL MUSICAL MYSTERY
PAPERCUTZ

#20 "High School Musical Mystery" 1

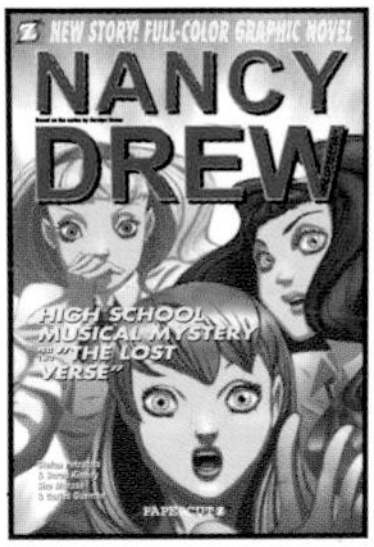
NEW STORY! FULL-COLOR GRAPHIC NOVEL
NANCY DREW
HIGH SCHOOL MUSICAL MYSTERY
THE LOST VERSE
PAPERCUTZ

#21 "High School Musical Mystery" 2

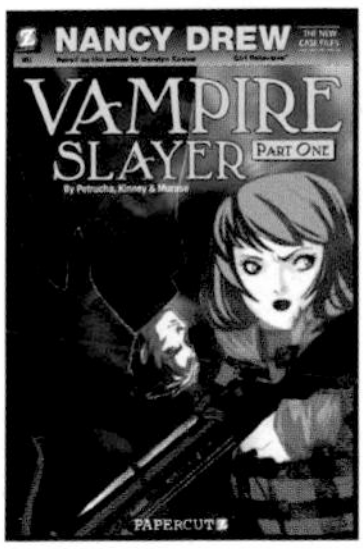
NANCY DREW
VAMPIRE SLAYER
PART ONE
By Petrucha, Kinney & Murase
PAPERCUTZ

The New Case Files #1 "Vampire Slayer" Part 1

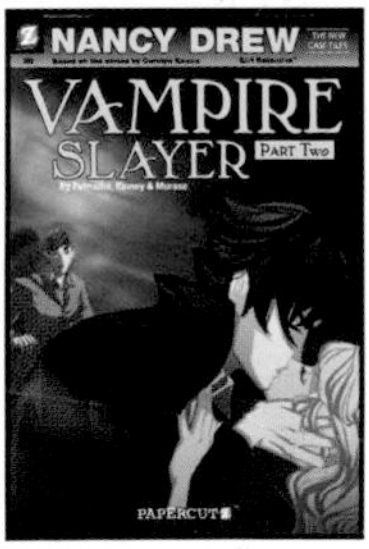
NANCY DREW
VAMPIRE SLAYER
PART TWO
By Petrucha, Kinney & Murase
PAPERCUTZ

The New Case Files #2 "Vampire Slayer" Part 2

Graphic Novels #12-19 are $7.95 in paperback, $12.95 hardcover. Graphic Novels #20 and #21 are $8.99 in paperback, $13.99 hardcover. NANCY DREW The New Case Files #1 and #2 are $6.99 in paperback, $10.99 hardcover. Please add $4.00 for postage and handling for the first book, add $1.00 for each additional book.

Please make check payable to NBM Publishing. Send to:

Papercutz, 40 Exchange Place, Ste. 1308 New York, NY 10005 * Or call 1-800-886-1223

www.papercutz.com

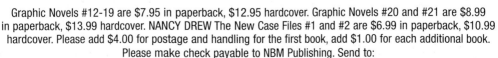

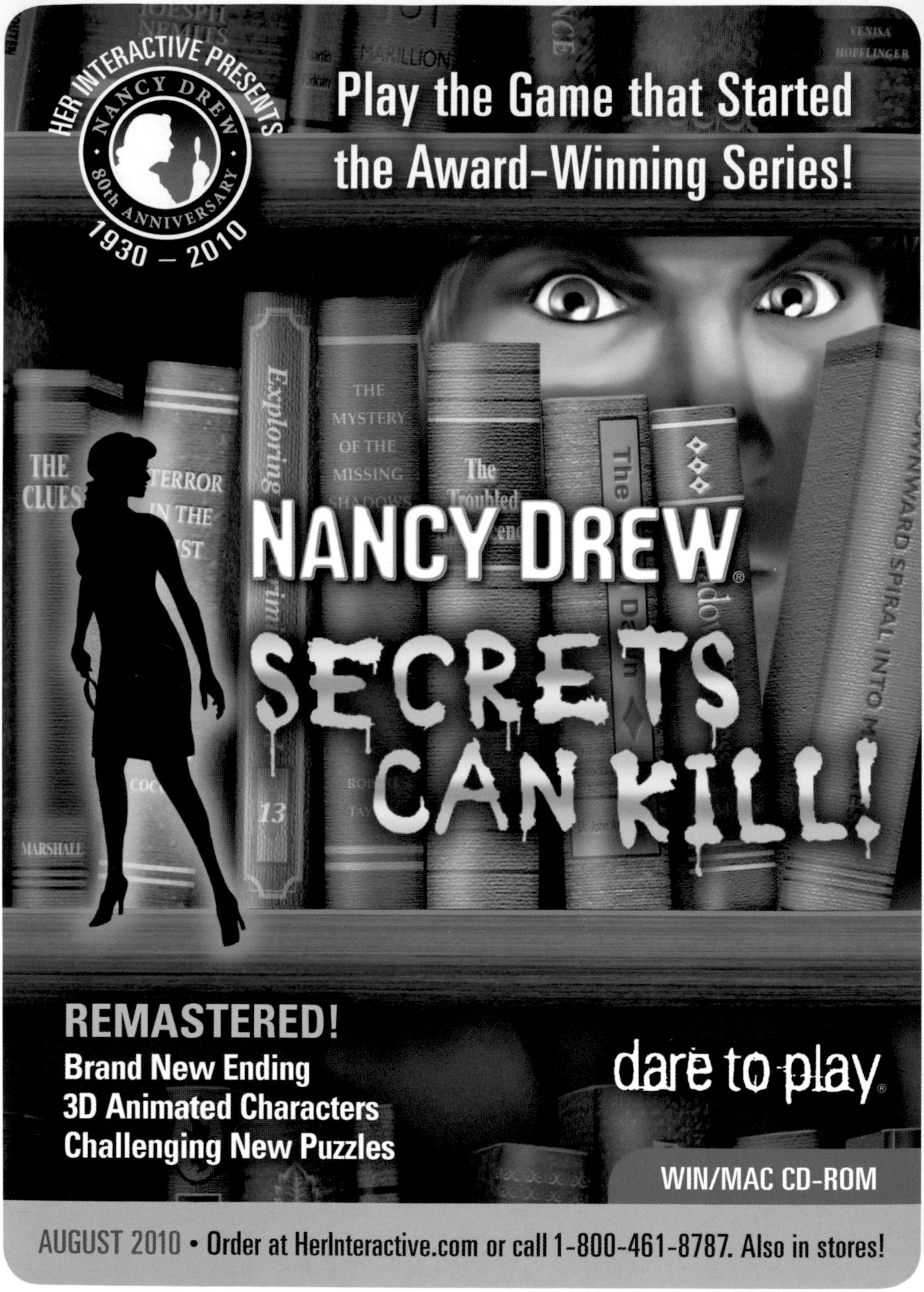
HER INTERACTIVE PRESENTS
NANCY DREW
80th ANNIVERSARY
1930 – 2010
Play the Game that Started the Award-Winning Series!
NANCY DREW®
SECRETS CAN KILL!
REMASTERED!
Brand New Ending
3D Animated Characters
Challenging New Puzzles
dare to play®
WIN/MAC CD-ROM
AUGUST 2010 • Order at HerInteractive.com or call 1-800-461-8787. Also in stores!

WATCH OUT FOR PAPERCUTZ™

Welcome to the thrilling third edition of the all-new NANCY DREW graphic novel series! I'm Jim Salicrup, Editor-in-Chief of Papercutz, publisher of great graphic novels for all-ages. Well—this is it! The answer to countless requests since we first started the NANCY DREW and THE HARDY BOYS graphic novels series way back in 2005! You wanted to see Nancy Drew team with Frank and Joe Hardy on a case, and though it may have taken a few years, it's finally here! Yes, Nancy Drew and The Hardy Boys—together again for the first time! While we've all enjoyed seeing the Girl Detective and The Undercover Brothers join forces to solve mysteries in print and on TV, this is the first time they've all gotten together in comics form! That makes this graphic novel an important event in the history of our favorite teen sleuths. And aren't you glad to be here to witness it?

Special thanks go to comics writing legend Gerry Conway for stepping in to write this historic encounter when regular NANCY DREW The New Case Files authors Stefan Petrucha and Sarah Kinney got too busy with other projects and were suddenly unavailable. That didn't stop our wondrous writers from passing on their story suggestions to Gerry, who did a great job of capturing the personalities of the NANCY DREW The New Case Files cast members. Also, thanks to Paulo Henrique, the regular artist on THE HARDY BOYS The New Case Files, for laying out our cover, and penciling the figures of Frank and Joe Hardy. Sho Murase and Carlos Guzman did their usual beautiful job completing the cover, and we hope you like it as much as we do!

If you're not already a follower of THE HARDY BOYS The New Case Files and enjoyed their appearance in these pages, may we suggest checking out their graphic novel adventures?

FULL-COLOR GRAPHIC NOVEL ADAPTATION
CLASSICS Illustrated
Deluxe
The Three MUSKETEERS
BY ALEXANDRE DUMAS
70th Anniversary Edition
Adapted by Morvan, Dufranne & Rubén
PAPERCUTZ

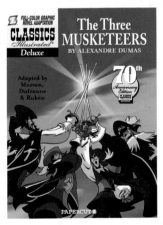

And speaking of adventure, we'd like to mention that there's an all-new comics adaptation of "The Three Musketeers" by Alexandre Dumas available now in CLASSICS ILLUSTRATED DELUXE #6. What makes this particular adaptation so special is not just the swashbuckling script, filled with action, romance, and intrigue by Jean David Morvan and Michel Dufranne or the spectacular artwork by Rubén—but the fact that CLASSICS ILLUSTRATED is celebrating its 70th Anniversary! Yes, back in October 1941, a new comicbook series launched called CLASSICS COMICS (which was later changed to CLASSICS ILLUSTRATED) and it adapted "The Three Musketeers" into comics form. Furthermore, this graphic novel is the biggest yet ever published by Papercutz—with the adaptation itself weighing in at 191 action-packed pages!

Now, don't ask us why we thought it would be appropriate to preview this all-new adaptation of "The Three Musketeers" in a graphic novel that reunited Nancy Drew, Frank, and Joe Hardy, but it sure seemed right to us.

And speaking of previews, we've also included a couple of mini previews of the latest all-new Papercutz super-stars—SYBIL THE BACKPACK FAIRY and ERNEST & REBECCA! Both titles make their debut in November, and we suspect you're going to love these girls (and Ernest too)!

There's so much going on at Papercutz these days that I can't possibly tell you everything on this one page, so may I suggest checking out our website at www.papercutz.com for the latest on DISNEY FAIRIES (featuring Tinker Bell), GARFIELD & Co, GERONIMO STILTON, PAPERCUTZ SLICES, THE SMURFS, and so much more!

So, until we meet again—keep sleuthing!

Jim

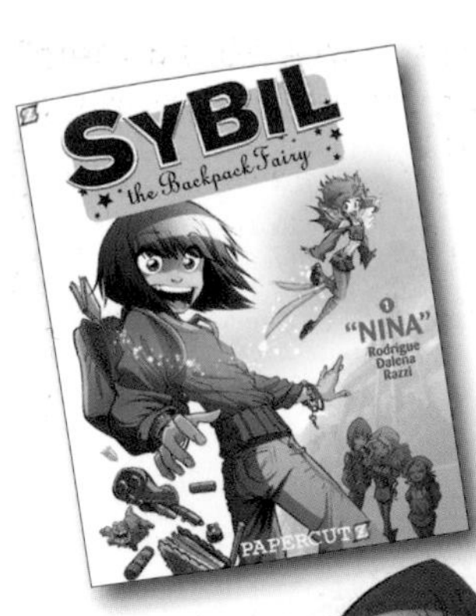
SYBIL
the Backpack Fairy
1
"NINA"
Rodrigue
Dalena
Razzi
PAPERCUTZ

Special preview of
SYBIL THE BACKPACK FAIRY #1 "Nina"

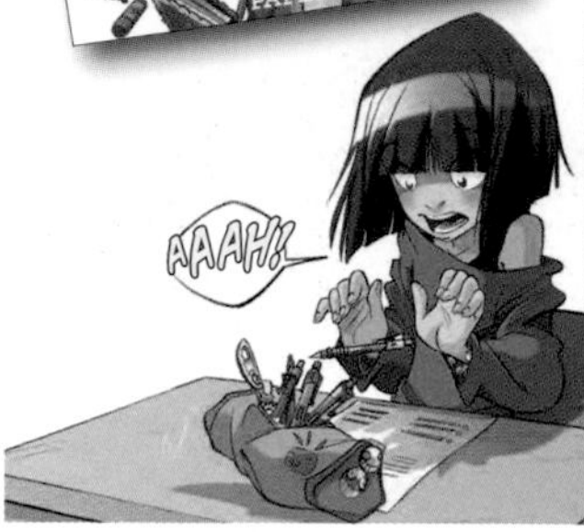
AAAH!

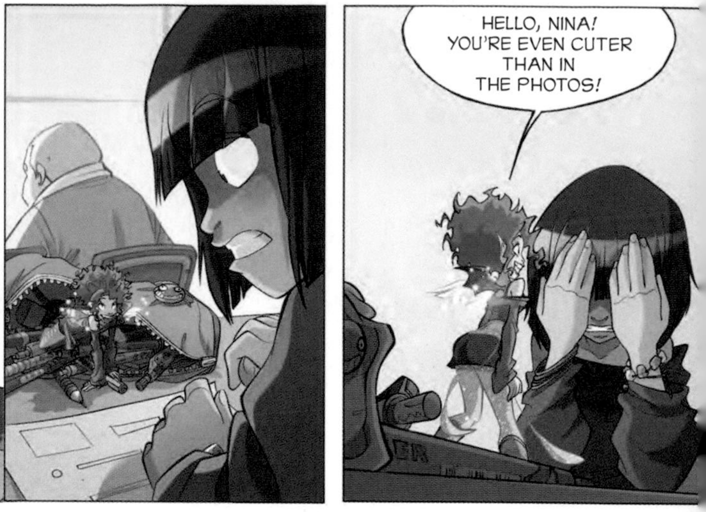
HELLO, NINA! YOU'RE EVEN CUTER THAN IN THE PHOTOS!

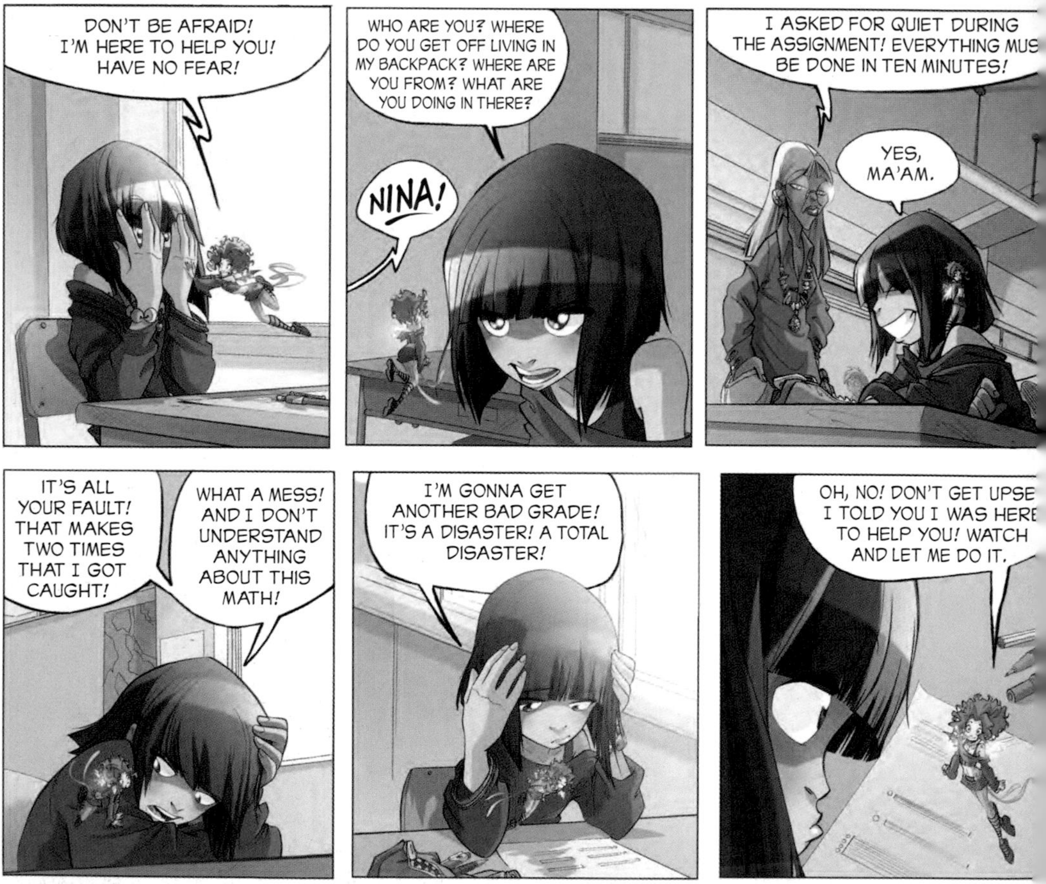
DON'T BE AFRAID! I'M HERE TO HELP YOU! HAVE NO FEAR!
WHO ARE YOU? WHERE DO YOU GET OFF LIVING IN MY BACKPACK? WHERE ARE YOU FROM? WHAT ARE YOU DOING IN THERE?
NINA!
I ASKED FOR QUIET DURING THE ASSIGNMENT! EVERYTHING MUS BE DONE IN TEN MINUTES!
YES, MA'AM.
IT'S ALL YOUR FAULT! THAT MAKES TWO TIMES THAT I GOT CAUGHT!
WHAT A MESS! AND I DON'T UNDERSTAND ANYTHING ABOUT THIS MATH!
I'M GONNA GET ANOTHER BAD GRADE! IT'S A DISASTER! A TOTAL DISASTER!
OH, NO! DON'T GET UPSE I TOLD YOU I WAS HERE TO HELP YOU! WATCH AND LET ME DO IT.

Don't miss SYBIL THE BACKPACK FAIRY #1 "Nina"
coming November 2011!

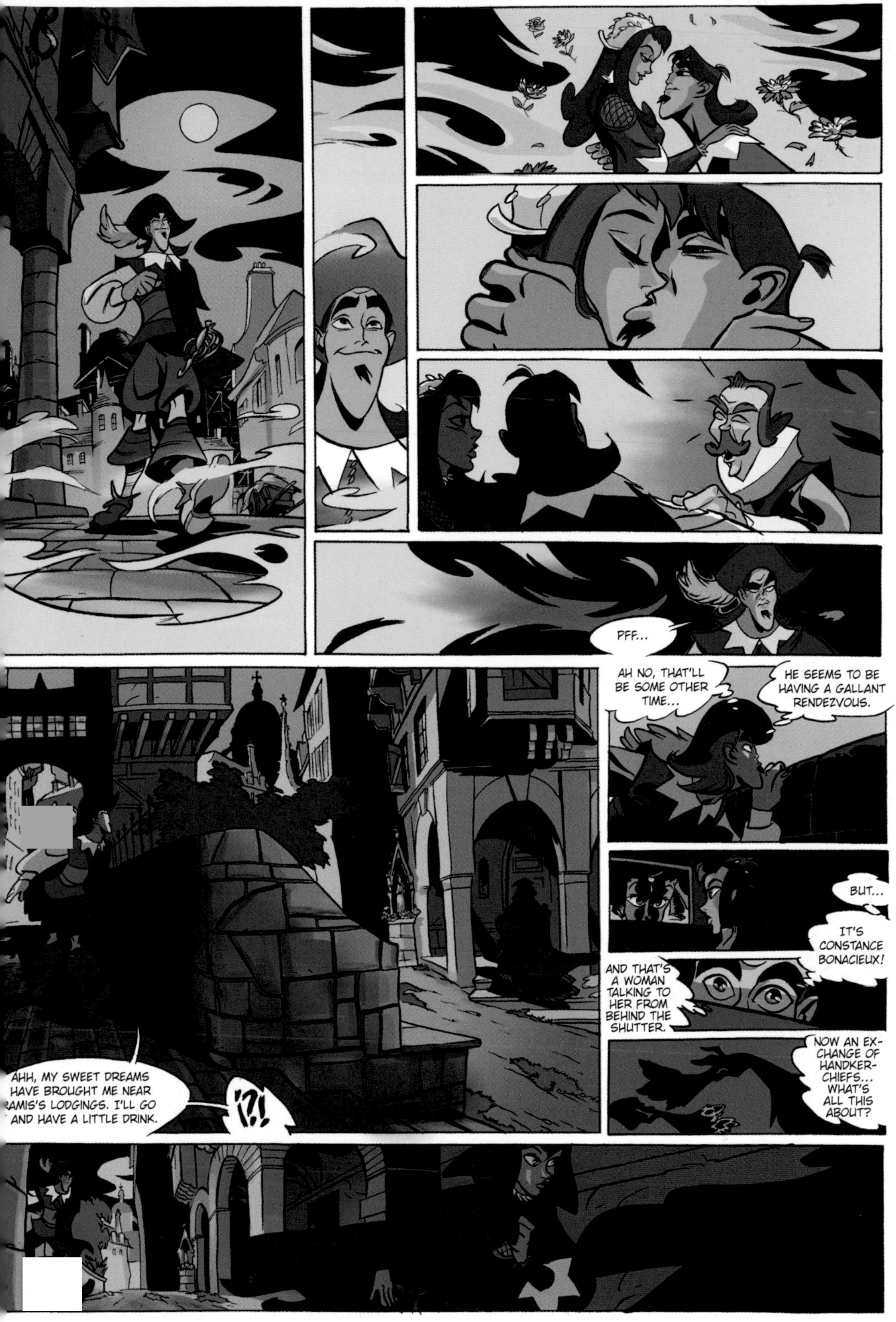
PFF...
AH NO, THAT'LL BE SOME OTHER TIME...
HE SEEMS TO BE HAVING A GALLANT RENDEZVOUS.
AHH, MY SWEET DREAMS HAVE BROUGHT ME NEAR ›AMIS'S LODGINGS. I'LL GO AND HAVE A LITTLE DRINK.
!?!
BUT...
IT'S CONSTANCE BONACIEUX!
AND THAT'S A WOMAN TALKING TO HER FROM BEHIND THE SHUTTER.
NOW AN EXCHANGE OF HANDKERCHIEFS... WHAT'S ALL THIS ABOUT?

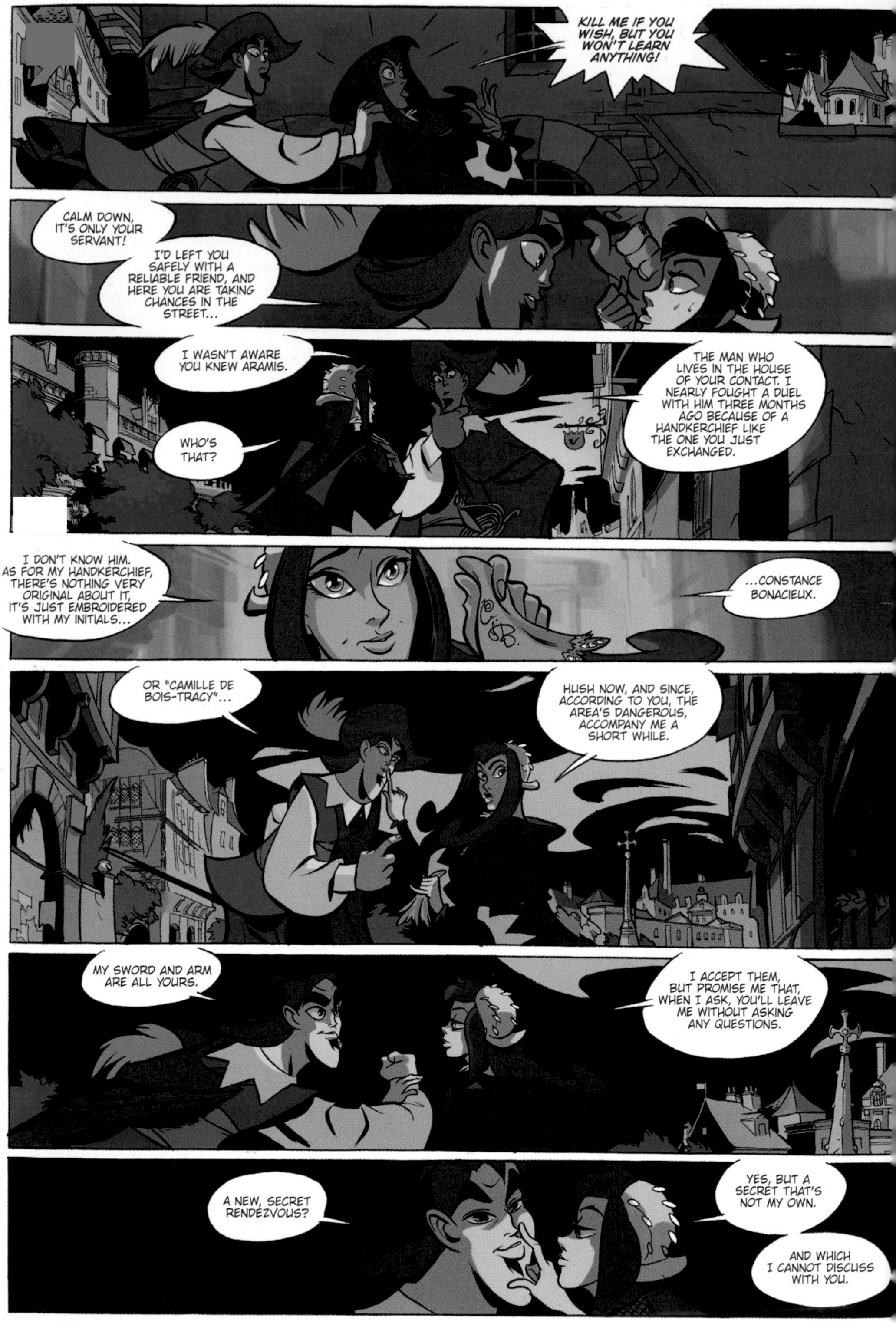
KILL ME IF YOU WISH, BUT YOU WON'T LEARN ANYTHING!
CALM DOWN, IT'S ONLY YOUR SERVANT!
I'D LEFT YOU SAFELY WITH A RELIABLE FRIEND, AND HERE YOU ARE TAKING CHANCES IN THE STREET...
I WASN'T AWARE YOU KNEW ARAMIS.
WHO'S THAT?
THE MAN WHO LIVES IN THE HOUSE OF YOUR CONTACT. I NEARLY FOUGHT A DUEL WITH HIM THREE MONTHS AGO BECAUSE OF A HANDKERCHIEF LIKE THE ONE YOU JUST EXCHANGED.
I DON'T KNOW HIM. AS FOR MY HANDKERCHIEF, THERE'S NOTHING VERY ORIGINAL ABOUT IT, IT'S JUST EMBROIDERED WITH MY INITIALS...
...CONSTANCE BONACIEUX.
OR "CAMILLE DE BOIS-TRACY"...
HUSH NOW, AND SINCE, ACCORDING TO YOU, THE AREA'S DANGEROUS, ACCOMPANY ME A SHORT WHILE.
MY SWORD AND ARM ARE ALL YOURS.
I ACCEPT THEM, BUT PROMISE ME THAT, WHEN I ASK, YOU'LL LEAVE ME WITHOUT ASKING ANY QUESTIONS.
A NEW, SECRET RENDEZVOUS?
YES, BUT A SECRET THAT'S NOT MY OWN.
AND WHICH I CANNOT DISCUSS WITH YOU.

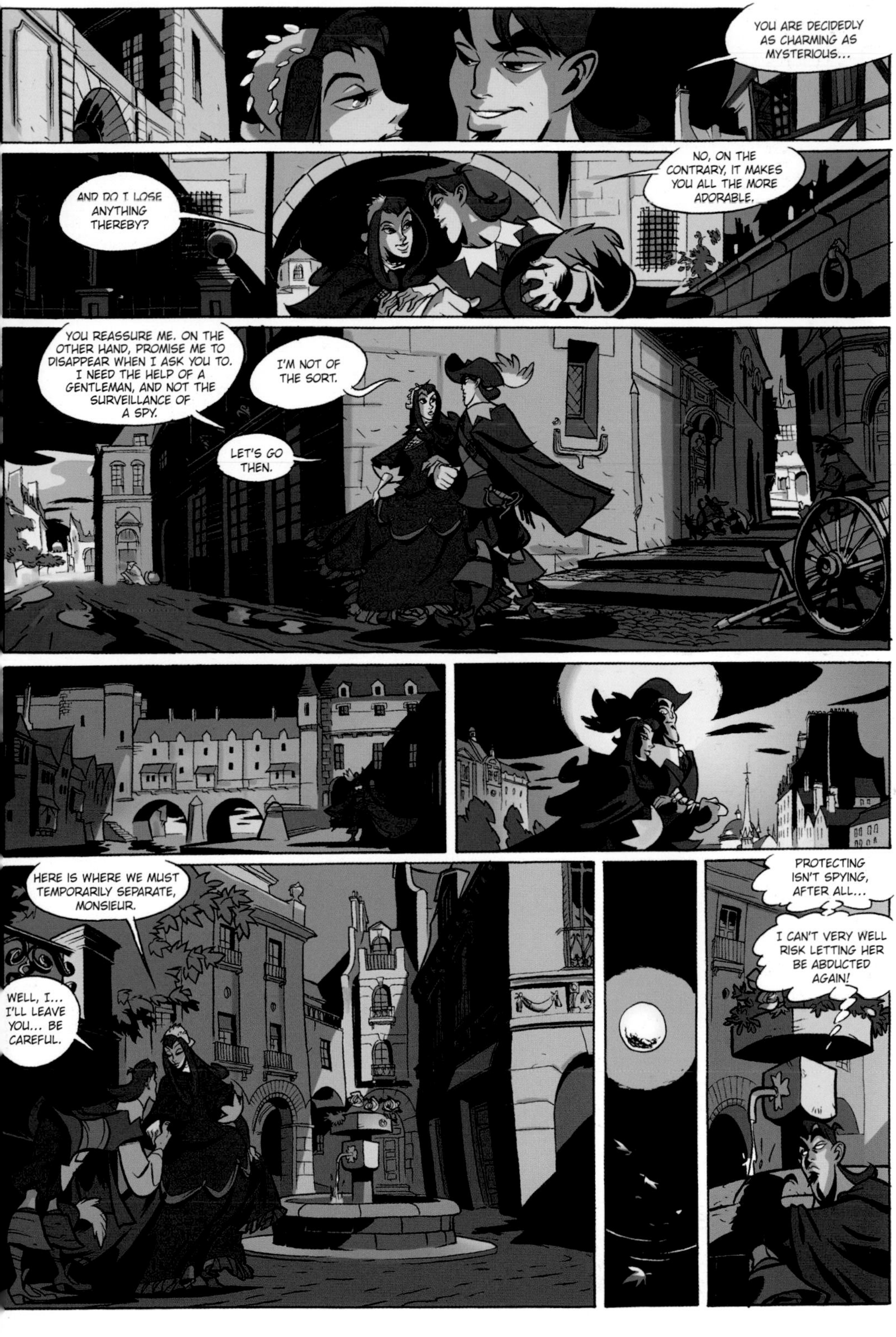
YOU ARE DECIDEDLY AS CHARMING AS MYSTERIOUS...
AND DO I LOSE ANYTHING THEREBY?
NO, ON THE CONTRARY, IT MAKES YOU ALL THE MORE ADORABLE.
YOU REASSURE ME. ON THE OTHER HAND, PROMISE ME TO DISAPPEAR WHEN I ASK YOU TO. I NEED THE HELP OF A GENTLEMAN, AND NOT THE SURVEILLANCE OF A SPY.
I'M NOT OF THE SORT.
LET'S GO THEN.
HERE IS WHERE WE MUST TEMPORARILY SEPARATE, MONSIEUR.
WELL, I... I'LL LEAVE YOU... BE CAREFUL.
PROTECTING ISN'T SPYING, AFTER ALL...
I CAN'T VERY WELL RISK LETTING HER BE ABDUCTED AGAIN!

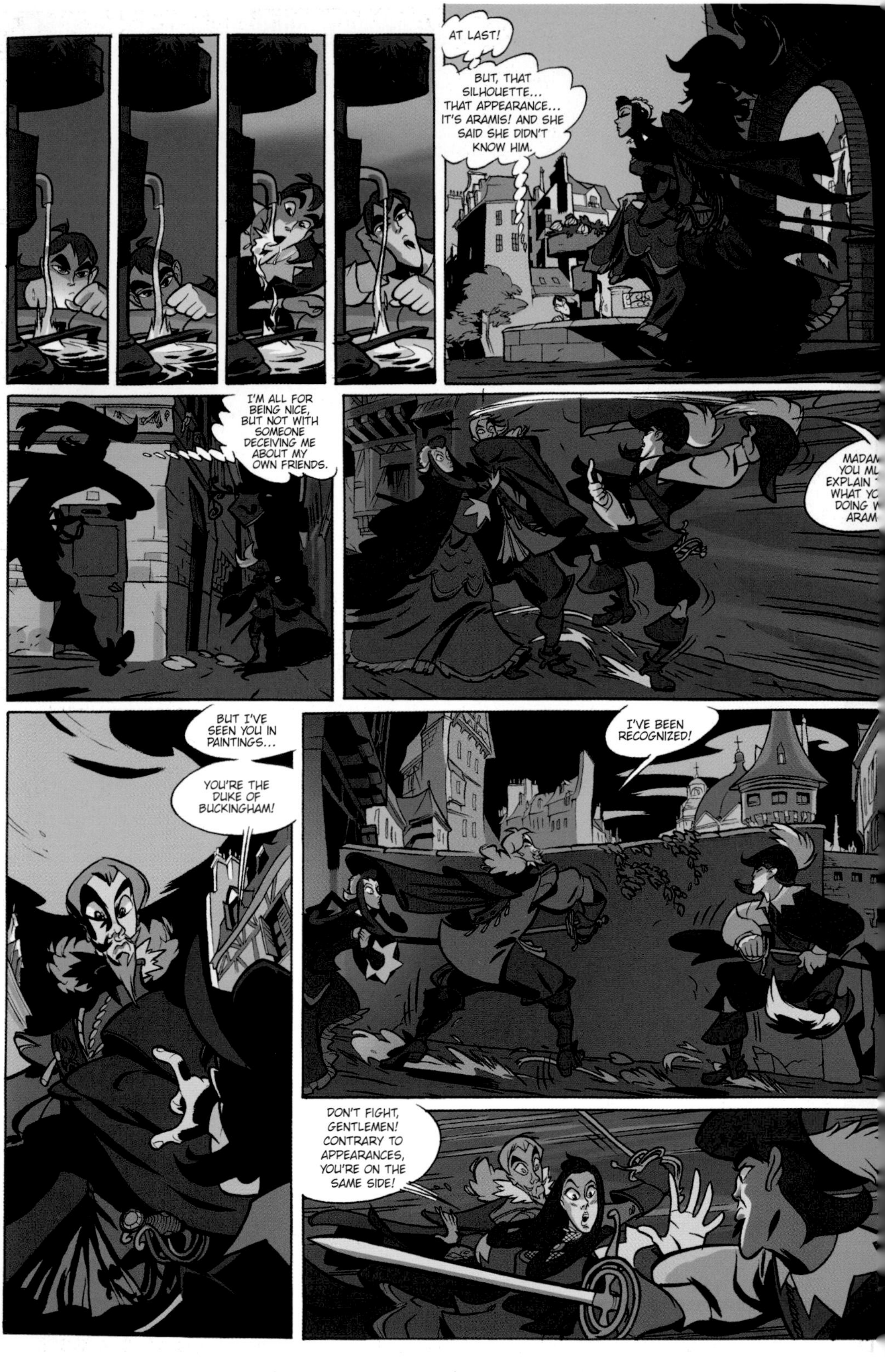
AT LAST!
BUT, THAT SILHOUETTE... THAT APPEARANCE... IT'S ARAMIS! AND SHE SAID SHE DIDN'T KNOW HIM.
I'M ALL FOR BEING NICE, BUT NOT WITH SOMEONE DECEIVING ME ABOUT MY OWN FRIENDS.
MADAM YOU MU EXPLAIN WHAT YO DOING W ARAM
BUT I'VE SEEN YOU IN PAINTINGS...
YOU'RE THE DUKE OF BUCKINGHAM!
I'VE BEEN RECOGNIZED!
DON'T FIGHT, GENTLEMEN! CONTRARY TO APPEARANCES, YOU'RE ON THE SAME SIDE!

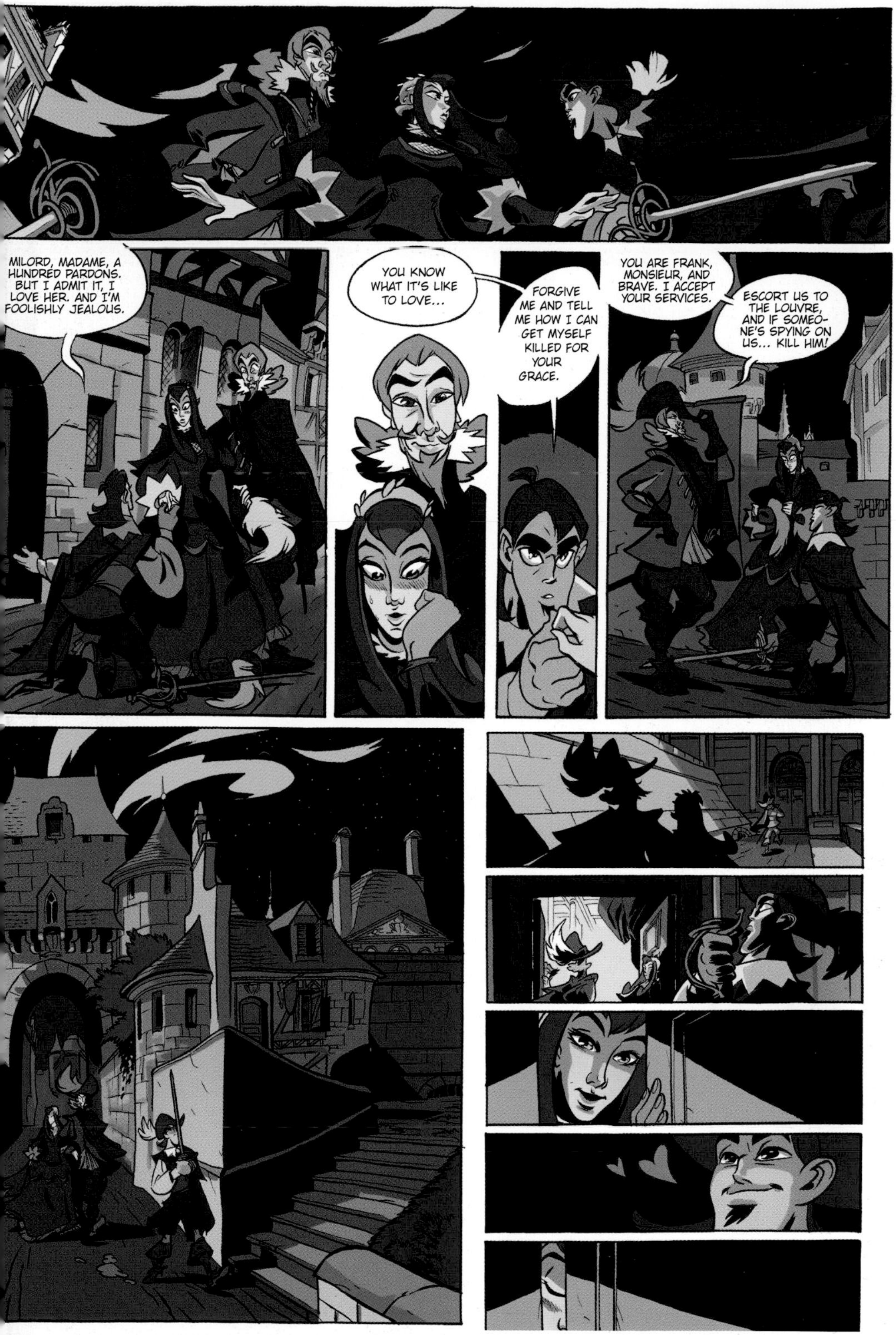
MILORD, MADAME, A HUNDRED PARDONS. BUT I ADMIT IT, I LOVE HER. AND I'M FOOLISHLY JEALOUS.
YOU KNOW WHAT IT'S LIKE TO LOVE...
FORGIVE ME AND TELL ME HOW I CAN GET MYSELF KILLED FOR YOUR GRACE.
YOU ARE FRANK, MONSIEUR, AND BRAVE. I ACCEPT YOUR SERVICES.
ESCORT US TO THE LOUVRE, AND IF SOMEONE'S SPYING ON US... KILL HIM!

Special preview of ERNEST & REBECCA #1 “My Best Friend is a Germ”

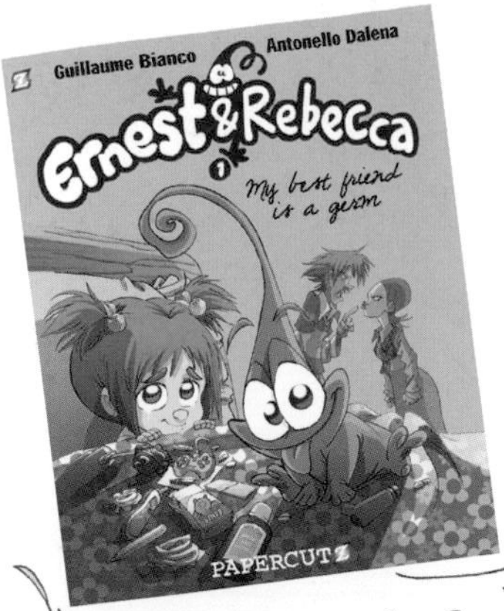
Guillaume Bianco
Antonello Dalena
Ernest & Rebecca
1
My best friend is a germ
PAPERCUTZ

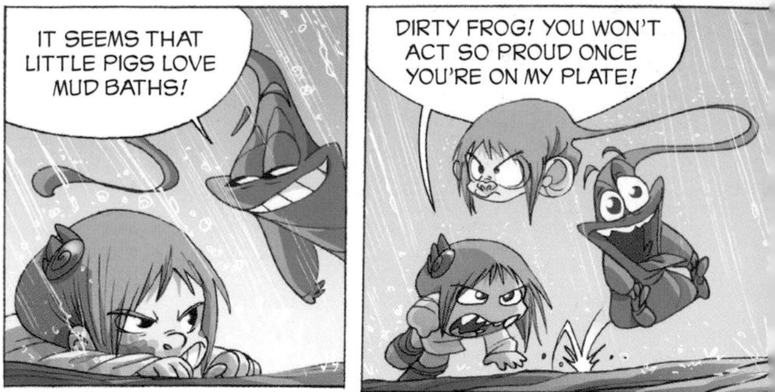
IT SEEMS THAT LITTLE PIGS LOVE MUD BATHS!
DIRTY FROG! YOU WON'T ACT SO PROUD ONCE YOU'RE ON MY PLATE!

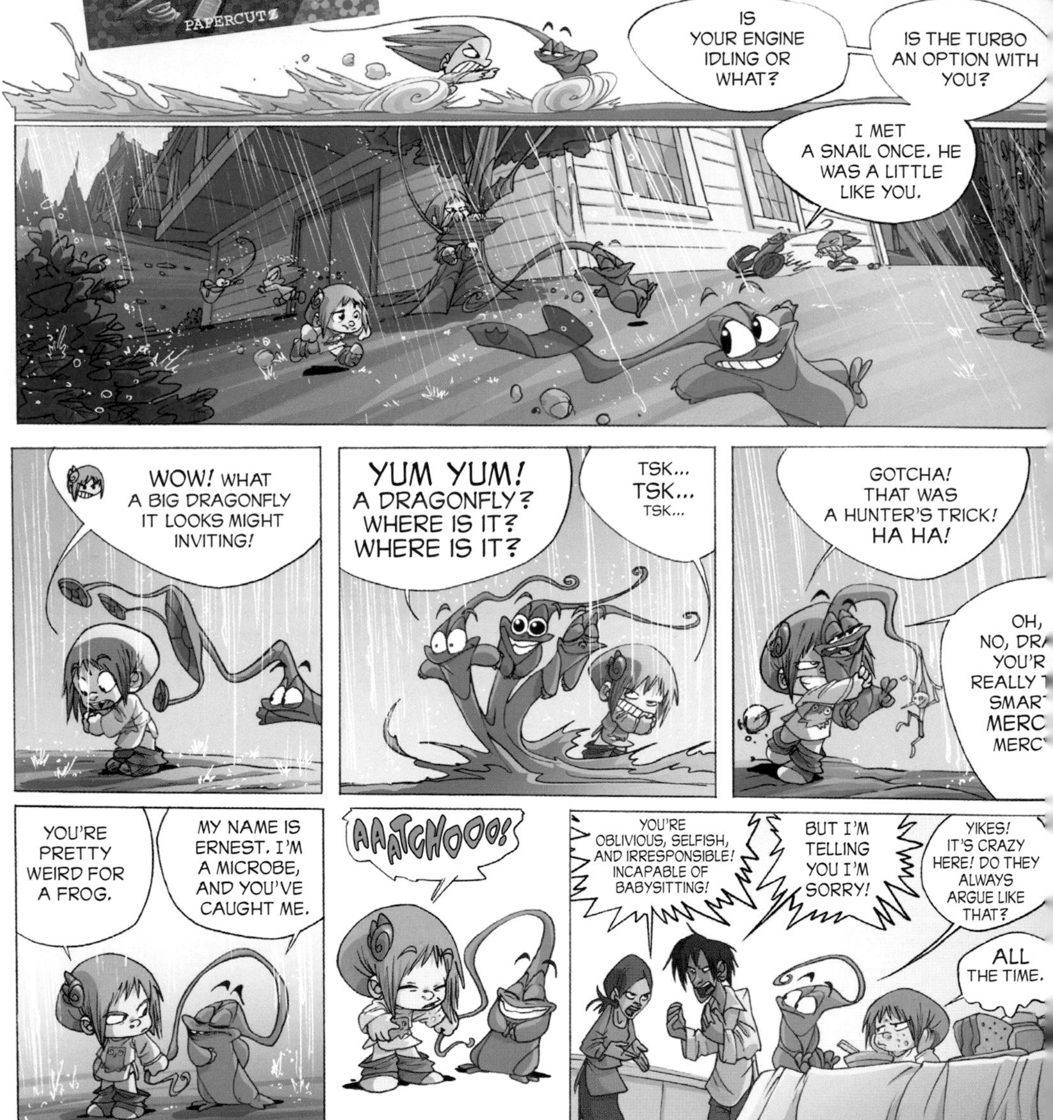
IS YOUR ENGINE IDLING OR WHAT?
IS THE TURBO AN OPTION WITH YOU?
I MET A SNAIL ONCE. HE WAS A LITTLE LIKE YOU.
WOW! WHAT A BIG DRAGONFLY IT LOOKS MIGHT INVITING!
YUM YUM! A DRAGONFLY? WHERE IS IT? WHERE IS IT?
TSK... TSK... TSK...
GOTCHA! THAT WAS A HUNTER'S TRICK! HA HA!
OH,
YOU'RE PRETTY WEIRD FOR A FROG.
MY NAME IS ERNEST. I'M A MICROBE, AND YOU'VE CAUGHT ME.
AAATCHOOO!
YOU'RE OBLIVIOUS, SELFISH, AND IRRESPONSIBLE! INCAPABLE OF BABYSITTING!
BUT I'M TELLING YOU I'M SORRY!
YIKES! IT'S CRAZY HERE! DO THEY ALWAYS ARGUE LIKE THAT?
ALL THE TIME.

Don't miss ERNEST & REBECCA #1 “My Best Friend is a Germ”
coming November 2011!